ALL FOR CAROLINE

ALL FOR CAROLINE

The only reason Megan Lacey takes the job of Speech Therapist at Kingscroft Cottage Hospital is to avenge her cousin Caroline whose hea.: had been broken some months before, by a callous young local doctor. Determined to seek him out and see justice done, Megan makes a terrible mess of things. To start with, she finds she's set her sights on the wrong man and, even worse, she discovers she is actually falling in love with the very same doctor who had caused her cousin so much anguish. What *has* she done? Was it really worth it – all for Caroline?

All For Caroline

by

Sarah Franklin

Dales Large Print Books
Long Preston, North Yorkshire,
BD23 4ND, England.

British Library Cataloguing in Publication Data.

Franklin, Sarah
    All for Caroline.

    A catalogue record of this book is
    available from the British Library

    ISBN   978-1-84262-686-3 pbk

First published in Great Britain in 1981 by Mills & Boon Ltd.

Copyright © Sarah Franklin 1981

Cover illustration © H Narborour by arrangement with
Allied Artists

The moral right of the author has been asserted

Published in Large Print 2009 by arrangement with
Jeanne Whitmee, care of Dorian Literary Agency

Dales Large Print is an imprint of Library Magna Books Ltd.

Printed and bound in Great Britain by
T.J. (International) Ltd., Cornwall, PL28 8RW

CHAPTER ONE

Megan parked her Mini in the only available space in the hospital car park and switched off the ignition with a sigh of relief. She had managed to find Kingscroft Cottage Hospital without any trouble at all. Map reading and following complicated directions had never been her strong suit but in her new job as a country speech therapist she would have to learn to be better at it.

She gathered up her handbag and jacket and got out of the car, but she was just locking the door when there was a loud hooting from behind her. Turning, she saw a red sports car, the driving seat of which was occupied by a large angry looking young man wearing sunglasses. He had an unruly shock of fair hair and he was waving his arms at her in an irritated manner.

'That's my parking space!' he bellowed. 'You'll have to move.'

Megan glanced round. Had she missed the customary name plate that said that the space was reserved for one of the hospital administrators? But no, there was no indication of any sort. She turned coolly to the occupant of the red car which was now revving furiously behind her.

'I'm sorry, but I was here first,' she said firmly. 'Why don't *you* look for another space?' She began to walk away but the man sprang out of his car and blocked her path. The first thought that came into her head was that it was quite incredible such a small car could accommodate a driver of such proportions. He was all of six feet tall and broad with it. The shock of coarse fair hair gave him a leonine appearance and as he snatched off his sunglasses Megan saw that his eyes were a deep and angry blue, like the sky before a thunderstorm.

'Just a darned minute!' he demanded in an accent she recognised immediately as Australian. 'I happen to be doctor on duty at this hospital. Who are you?'

Megan drew herself up to her full height – but she still found it necessary to tilt her head backwards in order to look at him. 'I also work here – or am about to,' she told him coldly. 'If you can show me anything that says this is your own personal parking space then I'll apologise and give it up. If not, then it's mine, I think!' She made to push past him but he stepped in front of her.

'You've got a hell of a cheek! I don't think I've seen you before. What's your name?'

She felt her colour rising as her normally gentle brown eyes looked back into the steely blue ones. 'If I have a cheek that matches yours,' she returned. 'It's clearly time you did meet me! You seem to have had your own way too long.' And, shaking with fury, she brushed him aside and headed for the out-patients' department where she hoped her friend Celia Morris would be waiting for her.

Celia was a medical secretary at the hospital who lived in the village of Little Avedon, six miles out of Kingscroft. She had replied to the advertisement Megan had placed in the local paper appealing for accommodation in the village and had recently moved out to Little Avedon after inheriting a cottage from her grandmother. But she could not afford its upkeep unless she took in a paying guest. The girls had arranged a meeting and had taken to each other on sight.

Megan had moved down to Little Avedon a week ago and having settled in she had come to the Cottage Hospital this afternoon at Celia's suggestion, to meet some of the people she would be working with and have

11

a look round generally. So far, she mused wryly as she made her way through the reception hall, so far she was doing rather badly!

At the desk Megan told the receptionist her name and her reason for being here. The girl smiled.

'Ah yes. I was told to expect you. Please come through.'

There were two other girls in the office besides Celia and Megan was greeted warmly, offered a comfortable chair and a steaming cup of coffee.

'Coffee's always on the go in here,' Celia told her. 'Being a cottage hospital there are no resident doctors and so no common room. Everyone sort of gravitates to this room for "tea and sympathy" as it were.'

'No resident doctors?' Megan queried.

Celia shook her head. 'No. Most patients admitted here are looked after by their own G.P. and the visiting consultants, though most of their cases are taken to Brinkdown General. Of course all the specialists hold clinics here, just as you will.' She laughed. 'Very different from what you've been used to, working in a big city hospital, I daresay. We're very informal here and we have to be ready to turn our hand to almost anything.

The staff are a marvellous bunch.'

At that moment the door opened to admit a girl in a white coat. She let her breath out on a long sigh and flopped into a chair.

'Phew! What a day! It's been all go. Any coffee going, Celia?'

Obligingly, Celia poured her a cup. 'Jane, I'd like you to meet our new speech therapist, Megan Lacey. Megan, this is Jane Lang, our physiotherapist.'

The two girls shook hands and then Jane began to regale them all with her stories about the past morning's work. She had an outrageous sense of humour and soon they were all rocking with laughter. Presently the door opened and a red-haired woman in the dark blue uniform of sister looked in.

'What's all the hilarity about?' she enquired in a brisk voice that carried more than a hint of Scottish brogue. 'I can hear you in "minor ops". May I remind you that this is a hospital, ladies, not a music hall!'

'Oh, come off it, Sister,' Jane said. 'I was just telling them about old Major Jackson and his fractured femur. All he seemed to be concerned about was how it would affect his old-time dancing!'

In spite of herself, Sister's lips twitched and to soften her still further Celia offered her a cup of coffee from the freshly made pot.

'By the way, Sister, this is Megan Lacey, our new speech therapist,' she said. 'This is Sister McNab, the mainstay of Kingscroft Cottage.'

Sister McNab blushed as she smiled across at Megan. 'Welcome to Kingscroft. Take no notice of us. We're all a bit mad here. And don't listen to a thing this lot tells you. They're given to wild exaggeration.' She swallowed her coffee hastily. 'Well, I'd better be going. Whenever I turn my back for a minute half of Kingscroft starts chopping off fingers and dropping babies on their heads!'

As she hurried out Jane pulled a face. 'And she accuses *us* of exaggeration!'

Celia smiled at Megan. 'Clinics will be starting soon. I'll just have time to show you your room and where everything is if you've finished your coffee.'

Together they moved towards the door, but just as Megan reached it it burst open, knocking her against the wall. A large young man filled the doorway, his tanned face damp with exertion.

'Have you got a quick coffee for a dying man, Celia?' he gasped. 'Some damned fool of a woman pinched my parking space and

I had to put the car across the road in the Council office car park. Sauce! I thought I was going to be late.'

Rubbing the place where her head had bumped the wall, Megan emerged from behind the door and glared at him. He had the grace to look slightly sheepish, but it was only momentary. His brows gathered as he returned her angry look.

'I hope you realise that you've wasted my valuable time!' he said.

'But not much of it – Doctor,' she returned coolly.

'Mr, actually.' Celia stepped between them. 'This is Mr Maitland, Megan. It's his E.N.T clinic this afternoon.' She looked uncertainly from one to the other. 'I – er – take it you've already met.' In the background Jane Lang stifled a giggle.

'Yes – we have met,' Megan said between tight lips.

'Miss Lacey is our new speech therapist,' Celia went on brightly. 'No doubt you'll be working together on the occasional case and of course you'll both have clinics here on the same – er – day.'

Two horrified faces turned to stare at her. 'The same day?' they chorused. One thought was in both their minds: That car park just

15

wasn't going to be big enough for both of them!

Megan salted the potatoes and lit the gas under the saucepan, glancing at her watch as she did so. Almost six o'clock. The meal should be ready by the time Celia got home. She took a biscuit from the jar on the dresser to ward off the pangs of hunger and sat down at the kitchen table.

It had not been a mere whim that she had chosen to live in the village of Little Avedon in the heart of the Cotswolds. As she looked out of the window she could see across the village green to the school with its quaint bell tower and picket fence; the school where her cousin Caroline had taught until the past Easter. It had been her first teaching job and she had loved it here – until a heartless man had brutally put a stop to her happiness.

Megan and Caroline had been brought up together ever since they were both five years old – when Caroline's parents had been killed in a tragic air crash. Although they were the same age Megan had always felt protective towards her cousin. She always seemed so vulnerable somehow, with her small fragile build and her huge innocent blue eyes. Even after she had grown up and completed her education she had seemed more infant-like to Megan than the children she taught.

When she had written to say she had met the man of her dreams, just six months after starting the job in the Cotswolds, Megan had been delighted. From the letter he had sounded exactly the right type for Caroline: a young doctor with a beautiful old house in the village. He sounded solid and dependable. He would look after Caroline and cherish her as she deserved. Then came the tearful phone call one night a few months later. Poor Caroline was quite distraught. It seemed that the whole thing had been a ghastly mistake. The doctor had never really loved her at all – let alone wanted to marry her. It was all over and she had given in her notice. She was going up to stay with friends in Scotland at the end of term, to recover from her broken heart. Angrily, Megan had demanded to know the name of the heartless doctor, but Caroline had refused to give it.

'I know you,' she said tearfully. 'You'd make trouble for him and I don't want that. He's a good doctor. He can't help it if he doesn't want me any more.'

'Don't go to Scotland, come home,' Megan had begged, but Caroline had been adamant. 'If I come home you'll get it all out of me, his name and everything. I still love him, Meg. I could never betray him.' And with that Megan had to be content.

She went restlessly from day to day, worrying about Caroline and wondering where she was and how she was feeling. Since her parents had died she had felt more responsible for her cousin than ever. The flat they had shared seemed to close in on her, but in spite of her repeated letters Caroline seemed determined to stay up north.

For some time she had been thinking of changing her job. She liked the idea of working in a country area instead of the city hospital where she had been since qualifying. Then, one evening when she was thumbing through one of the therapy journals her eye fell upon the advertisement: 'Cotswolds – Speech Therapist required for country area. How would you like to work among some of the most beautiful scenery in England? For further details please contact the area personnel department, Brinkdown, Gloucestershire.' That was the same authority that Caroline had worked for. Surely Little Avedon was no distance at all from Brinkdown?

Excitedly she got out the map to check. Slowly an idea had begun to evolve in her mind. If she were to apply for, and get, this job and having done that she were lucky enough to find digs in Little Avedon, she could do a quiet spot of detective work. Find this doctor person and somehow pay him back for what he had done to Caroline!

The more she thought about the idea, the more it appealed to her. No one would ever connect her with Caroline. Her parents had never formally adopted her so she had kept her own surname. There was no family resemblance either. In fact they could hardly have been more unalike for Megan's dark eyes and straight brown hair were in direct contrast to Caroline's bubbly blonde curls and ethereal quality. Exactly how she would 'get her own back' on Caroline's doctor, Megan wasn't very clear. The first step was to get the job, so she sat down there and then and sent off for the application forms.

What followed was almost a blur as she looked back on it all. There had been the interview with the Chief Medical Officer and the Area Speech Therapist, an agonising wait, and then the news that the job was hers. Finally, there had been digs to find and the business of sub-letting the flat, saying goodbye to friends and then moving into the cottage with Celia.

On the Saturday she arrived, Megan had explored the village and surrounding countryside in her Mini accompanied by Celia who pointed out all the places of interest then, after their evening meal, the girls had sat up till the small hours talking about themselves and their lives.

In Megan's case there was little to tell. Her life had been uneventful so far. She had been far too busy looking after Caroline to have much social life of her own. There had been her training course and the year and a half she spent working as a member of a team in the city hospital. All that had left her no time for frivolous pursuits at all. Even this move and the new life she was beginning were all on account of Caroline.

She realised very quickly that it was going to be difficult not to confide in Celia. She was such an open, friendly girl and had already told Megan most of her own hopes and fears for the future. On her left hand sparkled a diamond engagement ring. Her fiancé, she explained, was a purser in the Merchant Navy. She missed him very much, cherishing a fond hope that he would soon give up the sea and settle for a shore job.

The click of the gate brought Megan back to the present and she jumped up from the table. Celia was home. She'd better begin dishing up the meal. Although she'd only been at the cottage five days she felt completely at home, almost as though she'd been here all her life. This week she'd done most of the cooking and housework, but the girls had agreed that once she began work they would take it in turns.

'Mmm, that smells great!' Celia said as she opened the door and stepped into the kitchen.

'This is a habit I could well acquire! You're spoiling me, Megan.'

'Better make the most of it,' Megan grinned. 'From Monday the boot could be on the other foot. I daresay I'll quite often be late on the days when I'm working in the more remote places.' She popped the plates back into the oven while Celia took off her coat. 'It might be a good idea to prepare our meals in advance,' she said thoughtfully. 'We could have things like casseroles that could be stored in the fridge and heated up by whoever came in first.'

Celia smiled. 'I'm beginning to wonder what I did without you! You're a very practical lady, aren't you? I've a shrewd suspicion that I'm getting the best of this bargain.'

Megan pulled a face. 'Being what you call a "practical lady" doesn't sound very glamorous, but I suppose it's what comes of looking after my cousin for most of my life. If I start organising you more than you want just tell me, will you?'

Celia looked up as Megan put the steaming plate in front of her. 'Cousin? You never told me about her. Where is she now then?'

Megan felt her colour rise. Damn! She'd known it would slip out sooner or later. 'Oh she lives up north now,' she said casually. In such a small village it was highly likely that Celia had met Caroline while she was working here. She would have to be more careful.

But as Celia tucked hungrily into her food the subject soon turned to other matters.

'Oh, before I forget to tell you, I've arranged a little party on Saturday evening,' she announced. 'You met one or two of the people you'll be working with today and I thought it might be nice for you to meet some of the others – break the ice, so to speak.'

'What a nice idea,' Megan said smiling. 'Who have you invited?'

'Well, Sister McNab and Jane Lang for a

start because they're fun. Then there's Mrs Hadley, the secretary from Kingscroft Health Centre. Molly Edwards from the St Angela's School for the handicapped – you'll be coming into contact with her a lot, I daresay. I asked David Lattimer too. He's the village G.P. and I'm sure you'll like him, everyone does.'

Megan looked up sharply. 'He actually lives in the village then?'

'Oh yes, you must have noticed his house, Grey's Lodge. It's said to be the oldest house in the village and it has quite a history as well as being beautiful,' Celia told her.

Megan's heart was beating fast. 'Is he young?' she asked.

Celia smiled. 'Oh yes – and very eligible too. Thirty-ish and unmarried in spite of the efforts of the local mamas.'

Megan blushed. 'Oh! I wasn't asking for any particular reason – just interest.'

'You'll be interested all right,' Celia laughed. 'Just wait till you meet him. He's most attractive and charming too. Quite the darling of all the middle-aged ladies in Little Avedon – not to mention their daughters!'

Megan bit her lip hard. So that was it! There was little doubt about it. He must be the one who had jilted Caroline. Already she saw him as spoilt, conceited and arrogant. She almost said as much but stopped herself in time. She must play this with caution or she'd give the game away.

'Oh, there's one other guest,' Celia was saying. 'Jeff Maitland. He was there when I was inviting the others and before I knew it he'd sort of invited himself.'

Megan looked up vaguely. She had been so concerned with her own thoughts that she had hardly heard. 'Jeff Maitland – have I met him?'

'I should say so,' Celia smiled. 'Rather violently this afternoon, remember?'

Megan flushed at the memory. 'Him! Quite the most uncouth man I've ever met. He seemed to think he owned the hospital!'

'He's a bit outspoken at times,' Celia said. 'But his heart's in the right place.'

'His heart seemed to be firmly fixed under the bonnet of that noisy little sports car he drives this afternoon!' Megan retorted. 'He was really rude about what he insisted was *his* parking space.'

'The parking problem is a constant headache,' Celia sighed. 'And unfortunately there's no land available for enlarging the existing park. Everyone knows that space is unofficially Jeff Maitland's on Wednesday afternoons. You weren't to know.'

'In that case he might have been more polite about it,' Megan said. 'If he'd asked me nicely I would have moved. It was his attitude that annoyed me.'

Celia smiled. 'He was asking me about you after you'd left,' she said with a mischievous twinkle. 'Seemed to think you'd got character.'

Megan pursed her lips. 'Cheek, I believe he called it!'

'Not to me. He wanted to know all about you. That was when I was talking about the party – and the next thing I knew he was coming to it. I'm not quite sure how he did it.'

'Well, if you don't mind, I think I shall give him a wide berth,' Megan said dryly as she got up to fetch the pudding. 'I don't want to ruin the whole evening!' She did not add that she already had plans for getting acquainted with the eligible Doctor Lattimer.

'I've told everyone to bring their respective partners – married or otherwise,' Celia called. 'Jeff's been dating Staff Nurse Simms from Maternity, so he'll probably bring her.'

By seven o'clock on Saturday evening the table in the dining room was tastefully laid out with tempting snacks, bottles and glasses. The furniture was pushed back against the walls and the French windows were open, letting in the warm evening air.

Upstairs, the girls were putting the finishing touches to their appearance. Celia was in a pretty dress of blue chiffon, which accentuated her golden colouring, while Megan wore a stunning flame red dress which she had bought in a fit of extravagance in Brinkdown the previous afternoon. Its close-fitting bodice plunged deeply at front and back while the skirt flared gently over her slender hips. She was just applying the lipstick she had chosen to match the dress when the front door bell rang. Celia let out a howl.

'A buckle has just come off my sandal,' she called.

'It's all right, I'll go.' Megan ran lightly down the stairs.

'Tell whoever it is I'll be down in a minute,' the other girl called. 'And offer them a drink!'

Through the bobble-glass panel in the front door Megan could see that the early arrival was male. She had rather hoped it might be Sister McNab or someone she had already met. But it couldn't be helped. She opened the door with a smile and found herself looking at one of the most handsome faces she had ever seen.

'Ah – you must be Megan Lacey.' He held out his hand. 'I'm David Lattimer, the local G.P. – for my sins.'

Megan shook the hand he offered feeling slightly chastened. He was not what she had imagined at all. She had visualised him as tall and dark with a cynical curving mouth and maybe a moustache. He couldn't have been more different. A little over average height, he had brown wavy hair and humorous grey eyes. He was impeccably dressed in a dark grey suit and blue shirt. As Megan closed the door he smiled at her.

'It'll be good to have a speech therapist in the area again,' he said. 'We don't seem to have attracted anyone to this area since the last one left to be married. I'm sure you'll find you're very welcome wherever you go.'

She returned his warm smile. 'I've certainly found the people I've met so far very kind and friendly,' she said. 'Do come in and have a drink. Celia will be down in a minute.'

As she poured him a drink she pondered over the initial surprise she had felt on meeting him. He didn't seem at all the sort to trifle with a girl's affections. Still, first impressions were not always accurate. Turning, she handed him the glass.

'Are you on call this evening, Doctor?'

He frowned. 'David, please. I hate formality when I'm off duty. Actually the doctor in the next village takes it in turns with me to be on call at weekends. We have to have some social life, even here in the depths of the country.' He looked at her, his head slightly on one side. 'Aren't you going to join me?'

She raised an eyebrow. 'Join you?'

He held out his glass. 'In a drink.'

'Oh – of course.' Feeling slightly foolish she turned away to pour herself a glass of sherry, then held it up. 'Here's to the people of Little Avedon,' she said.

'No, here's to you, Megan,' he corrected. 'And all the good I'm sure you're about to do.'

As she sipped the sherry she felt her cheeks burn. If he only knew what it was she intended to do here! What would he think then?

Celia made her appearance and David stood up to greet her. Then the door bell rang again and the guests began to arrive one by one. Megan gave a sigh of relief. Her conversation with David Lattimer had been disarming to say the least, yet she was determined not to have her opinion of him changed. That boyish charm was obviously his stock in trade.

As the party got under way the guests spilled out onto the tiny patio and lawn with their drinks. Laughter and conversation filled the air, the evening was a success. Everyone wished Megan well in her new job and they all echoed David Lattimer's sentiment that she was badly needed. It was about nine o'clock when the door bell rang again. Megan had come inside to replenish some glasses and she went through to the hall, wondering who it could be at this late hour. She had thought everyone had arrived.

Jeff Maitland filled the doorway with his bulk, his fair hair more tousled than ever.

'Sorry to be late. I had a puncture,' he told her succinctly. 'Boy! Could I use a drink!' He stepped into the little hallway, seeming to dominate it with his presence. 'Well–' He looked at her. 'Lead me to it, Megan m'love. What are you waiting for – Christmas?'

She had just opened her mouth to make a sharp rejoinder when she felt a movement behind her. Turning, she saw a beautiful girl with red hair still standing in the porch.

'Oh, I'm so sorry,' she stammered. 'I didn't know–'

'No!' The girl stared past her at Jeff Maitland. 'Manners aren't exactly Jeff's strong suit. I'm Julia Simms and I'm *supposed* to be with him!'

'Megan Lacey.' Megan held out her hand, smiling apologetically at the girl. 'Please come in.'

'Oh, come off it you two!' Jeff exploded. 'Why are you English so damned prissy and formal? It's a party, isn't it? Not a wake!' And so saying he disappeared into the throng of guests leaving them looking at each other speechlessly.

Feeling sorry for the girl, Megan made sure that she had a drink and someone to talk to before she mingled again with the guests. She had not yet had time for a proper conversation with David Lattimer and she was determined that the evening should not go by without her getting to know him better. But as she was searching the crowd for him she felt a tap on her shoulder and turned to find herself face to face with him.

'Ah, there you are,' he smiled. 'You've been so much in demand all evening that I haven't had a minute to talk to you. Maybe we could take a stroll down Celia's delightful garden?'

Dusk was falling as they walked across the lawn and through the little gate in the hedge. Beyond was an old English flower garden, complete with crazy-paved paths and a riot of early summer flowers. The warm evening air was heavy with their scent – wallflower, lily-of-the-valley, stocks. David breathed deeply and smiled.

'Delicious, isn't it?' He took her arm. 'I believe Celia's grandfather planted it all over fifty years ago. It's a good thing she enjoys gardening herself.'

Megan nodded. 'She loves this old cottage. I can see why. Old houses have so much more character.'

He smiled down at her. 'You must come and see my house and garden. They're supposed to be the oldest in the village. They have an interesting history too. A woman who was convicted for witchcraft is supposed to have lived there in 1673. She was sentenced to be hanged but a week before the sentence was carried out she predicted that an accident would happen to the local Lord of the Manor. She said that he would be thrown from his horse and that she would be the only person able to restore him to life.'

'What happened?' Megan asked, fascinated.

'It came about just as she had said it would,' he told her. 'The man lay unconscious for two days until his distraught wife demanded that old Matty should be released and brought to him. Matty asked to be taken to her house first so that she could prepare medicine and poultices from the special herbs she grew in her garden, then she was taken to the Manor where she effected her miraculous cure. Two days later the Lord was quite himself again.'

'And what happened to Matty?' Megan asked.

'She was pardoned. One of the few English witches who ever was. Of course there were those who said it was her very sorcery that brought the whole thing about, but luckily the Lord and Lady of the Manor would have none of it. She lived unmolested for the rest of her life and received a stipend of a shilling a week.'

Megan laughed. 'They knew how to be generous in those days!'

David nodded. 'It may not sound much, but think of the peace of mind she must have enjoyed. You must come and see her garden. It still flourishes. Why not come across and have a drink with me next week – what about Monday?'

'I'd like that very much,' she replied. And she meant it. This young doctor with his beguiling charm was obviously attracted to her. Maybe *that* was one way of avenging Caroline's broken heart. Anyway, it was worth a try.

CHAPTER TWO

The first working day in Megan's new job was a whirl of activity. At first she was nervous. Working as she had, as part of a team, she had been used to having reassurance at hand such as another therapist with more experience than she to consult in times of doubt. How would she cope on her own? That was the question uppermost in her mind on that first morning as she drove her Mini out to Brinkdown Health Centre where she was to take her first clinic. But she need not have worried. That morning's clinic was for children and as soon as she began work with them she forgot her apprehension.

Working in a big city hospital she had had experience of most of the routine problems as well as the more unusual ones. She had always liked children and was usually able to establish a good relationship with them in a short time. Her small patients that morning included some with delayed language problems as well as the common articulation difficulties and she was delighted to find that the centre possessed a Language Master machine like the one she had been used to, where each child could practice with his or her own tape.

The morning flew past and by the time the lunch break came round she felt well pleased with the start she had made. The children seemed to have enjoyed their visit, the work and 'games' she had given them. The mothers too had seemed eager to co-operate, promising to keep up the good work at home till next time. Only one woman, the mother of a little boy with a severe stammer, hung back afterwards, a doubtful, worried look on her face. Megan smiled at her.

'Did you want to talk about Damion, Mrs Shaw?' she prompted.

The young woman nodded eagerly and followed Megan back into her room where she sat down in the chair opposite Megan's.

'It's just that he doesn't seem to be getting any better,' she said. 'I thought it might help if you knew a bit more about him. He hasn't always stammered, you see. It started when his Granny died – my mother. He was very close to her, she used to have him while I was at work. The shock of losing her seemed to bring on the stammer. Then soon after that he started school and the other children teased him – well, you know how thoughtless kids are. The doctor says it's only nerves and that he'll grow out of it in time.' She shook her head. 'Sometimes I wonder though.'

Megan nodded understandingly. 'I know. It's very distressing when you feel there's nothing you can do to help. I believe there is something we might try in Damion's case though. It's called an Edinborough Masker. It means having a tiny microphone taped to the throat, connected to an equally tiny amplifier – something like a deaf-aid, in the ear. The idea is that the microphone picks up the vibration from the larynx and conveys it to the ear so that the word the patient is trying to say becomes "unstuck" as it were.'

Mrs Shaw frowned. 'It all sounds a bit far fetched,' she said doubtfully. 'Does it really work?'

'It may sound strange, but it does,' Megan assured her. 'But I must warn you that it's not a cure. It's benefit lies in the fact that it encourages confidence in the speaker, so that in a case like Damion's it could well help him to overcome his stammer more quickly.'

Damion's mother looked more cheerful. 'I see. This microphone you mentioned, and the earpiece, wouldn't it be unsightly, something else for the other kids to pick on?'

Megan shook her head. 'They're both extremely small. The microphone would be hidden by his collar and the ear-piece is close fitting. I feel sure it wouldn't bother him. What do you say – would you like to try it?'

The woman nodded. 'Oh yes, please. It's certainly worth a try.'

'Right.' Megan drew her note pad towards her. 'I'll put a recommendation in the report I shall be sending to your G.P. In the meantime, don't forget to bring him to the centre next time, will you. It all helps.'

'I don't think I've a chance of keeping him away,' Mrs Shaw said with a smile as she got up. 'Those games you played with him were a real hit. I can see I'm going to be kept busy from now on.'

After a snack lunch Megan was to drive to a school for handicapped children to work for the rest of the day, but on the way she had a house call to make on a patient referred to her by Mr Dobbs, the neurologist at Brinkdown General. Peter Forbes had been the victim of a particularly nasty motor bike accident. He had suffered brain damage and, as a result, was partially paralysed. He had also lost his power of speech. His doctor reported that although the boy was responding well to the physiotherapist's attempt to exercise his limbs, he would make no attempt to speak at all.

Megan knocked on the door of the trim council house and a moment later found herself looking into a pair of anxious blue eyes. She introduced herself.

'Oh, please come in, Miss Lacey,' Mrs Forbes invited. 'To be honest, you're our last hope. Peter's out in the garden. He's doing so well in everything else – but the speech–' she broke off, shaking her head. 'It was such a shock to him to find he couldn't speak after the accident. At first he used to get so frustrated you could tell that all he wanted to do was to smash things. Since he's been home from the hospital though he just seems to have given up.' She shrugged helplessly. 'Do you think there's any hope at all?'

Megan glanced out of the window at the good-looking boy in the wheelchair. 'According to the doctor's report there's every hope, Mrs Forbes,' she said. 'But Peter must *want* to speak. It really all depends on him. One thing you must try to avoid is anticipating his every want. If he never *needs* to ask for things he won't bother to try.'

Mrs Forbes nodded. 'I see, yes that makes sense. I suppose I have spoiled him a bit since he came home. We were so thankful just to have him back. They didn't think he'd live through the night when it happened, you know. A nightmare, it was!'

'Well all that is over now,' Megan said briskly. 'And the next thing is to get him back to normal as soon as possible. May I see him now, please?'

In the sunny little garden Peter Forbes sat reading a science fiction magazine on the pocket handkerchief-sized lawn. He was a solemn faced, handsome boy of about nineteen.

'He can use his hands again now,' his mother said proudly. 'Yesterday he weeded the flower beds for me with the hoe.'

Peter glanced up but when he saw Megan his face clouded and he held his magazine up high in a deliberate snub. His mother clicked her tongue.

'Oh dear. I'm afraid he does this with everyone who tries to help. It's not very encouraging, is it?'

Megan sat down in the deckchair that had obviously been vacated by Mrs Forbes. 'Hello, Peter. I'm Megan Lacey and I'm the new speech therapist.'

The boy ignored her and his mother shook her head, fussily apologising again for his rudeness. Megan looked up at her.

'Mrs Forbes, I wonder if I might beg a cup of tea?' she asked. 'I didn't have time for one with my lunch.'

Mrs Forbes threw up her hands. 'Oh, you poor girl! Going without so that you could come and visit us. Of course I'll make you one. We were just going to have one anyway.' And she hurried off into the house.

Megan sat back in the deckchair with a sigh. Asking for the tea was the only way she could think of to be alone with Peter for a few minutes. She glanced at the dark eyebrows drawn together which were all she could see above the covers of the magazine. She guessed that he wasn't taking in a word of it.

'I'm sorry to disturb you, Peter,' she ventured. 'But I must say it's pleasant to sit here in your nice garden.' She glanced at him. 'Shall I tell you something? This is my very first day in a new job. It's the first time I've ever worked entirely on my own and I'll confess to you that I'm rather nervous. It's important to me, you see, to show that I can cope – to have something to show for my efforts.' She laughed. 'I expect you think I'm daft.'

The magazine was lowered a couple of inches and a pair of solemn brown eyes looked into hers for the first time. Slowly, he shook his head from side to side. Megan smiled.

'You don't? Oh, that's marvellous. I'd love to help you find that voice of yours again, Peter. That's what it would be, you know – *finding* it, because it's still there somewhere.'

Peter opened his mouth, then closed it again, biting his lip.

'There's a clinic for patients like you at the Health Centre on Thursday mornings,' she went on. 'Some people have had even worse accidents than you if you can believe that, and some have had operations. I wish you'd come. It would be nice for you to meet the others and make friends. Will you? I could arrange for transport.'

Again he bit his lip, his eyes clouding again, then he raised the magazine once more to hide his face, dismissing her. Megan sighed.

'Oh dear. My first day and already I've drawn a blank.' She stood up. 'I'll go and help your mother with that tea. I wish you'd come to the clinic, Peter, even if it was just to have a look round. But I can't make you, can I?' She began to move towards the house but she had not gone far when a sound made her stop. She turned. Peter had laid down his magazine and was looking at her, his eyebrows raised. He nodded with firm deliberation.

'You'll come – next Thursday?' she asked him, holding her breath. He nodded again. 'Thank you, Peter,' she said delightedly. 'You've done me a favour. Now we'll see whether I can do you one, shall we?'

In the Forbes' kitchen she told Mrs Forbes what she had achieved. 'Your son can learn to speak again,' she said. 'He's given up temporarily because he can't make his voice-producing equipment form the words and sounds that are in his mind. He's embarrassed and frustrated by what comes out so he's decided not to try any more. It's called dysarthia and as well as treatment at the clinic a lot of work must be done at home. So I'd like you to attend the clinic with him on Thursdays. Will this be possible?'

Mrs Forbes' face was wreathed in smiles. 'Nothing would please me more,' she said. 'It'll be wonderful to be able to help him speak again!'

Megan smiled back. She thought so too.

By the time she got home that evening Megan was quite tired. She had hardly stopped all day and as she let herself into the cottage she sniffed appreciatively at the appetising aroma coming from the kitchen where Celia was preparing their evening meal. Opening the door, she put her head round it.

'Mmm, smells marvellous!'

'Well it should do, it's the casserole you made last night,' Celia told her. 'I'm only the one who's heating and eating!'

Megan lowered herself into a chair with a sigh. 'I'm starving and exhausted. I think I'll have a nice hot bath and an early night,' she said longingly.

Celia glanced at her. 'Oh, like that, was it?'

'Oh no, it was terrific really,' Megan assured her. 'Just a bit nerve-racking, like all first days. I'll be fine once I've settled in.'

Celia strained the potatoes and began to dish up. 'I hope you haven't forgotten that you have a date tonight,' she said.

Megan gasped. In all the excitement she had completely forgotten that this was the night she was invited to David Lattimer's.

'Heavens, of course,' she said. 'I'm going to Doctor Lattimer's to look at his herb garden.'

'Herb garden!' Celia laughed. 'That's a new one! Makes a change from etchings, I must say!' She put Megan's plate in front of her and sat down opposite. 'Eat up while it's hot, as my mother used to say.'

Megan looked at her thoughtfully as she ate. 'Tell me about David Lattimer,' she said at last. 'Why is he still single, for instance? In my experience most young G.P.s are married. It can't be on account of his looks.'

Celia shrugged. 'I've no idea. I know it's not for the want of female admirers.'

'Anyone in particular?' Megan probed.

The other girl shot her a quizzical glance. 'Why – are you smitten?'

'Of course not. I hardly know him!' Megan said blushing hotly. 'I'm just curious, that's all.'

Celia laughed. 'All right. I'm only teasing. No, all David's girl friends have been short-lived, I think. It's not all honey after all, being the wife of a country G.P. I imagine one would have to be very dedicated as well as very much in love.'

Megan finished her meal without further comment. No one could have been more in love than Caroline, to judge from her letters. Why then, had David Lattimer treated her so cruelly? Well, with any luck she would gather some clues tonight!

Grey's Lodge was a small but solid house on the edge of the village. It was built of mellow Cotswold stone and had deep set, mullioned windows with leaded panes which twinkled in the evening sunshine. Megan rang the bell and almost immediately the front door was opened by a smiling middle-aged woman.

'You'll be Miss Lacey,' she said. 'I'm Mrs Jenkins, Doctor's housekeeper. He told me to expect you. Won't you come in. He's just been called out but he doesn't expect to be kept long.' She showed Megan into a pleasant room with white walls and a low beamed ceiling. The long windows were open and the summer scents from the garden filled the room.

'Oh, how lovely!' Megan exclaimed. 'I wouldn't mind being a patient myself if the doctor's surgery was in such a beautiful place.'

'Oh, surgery's not here,' Mrs Jenkins told her. 'This is just Doctor's home. Surgery's in the centre of the village, next door to the post office.'

'I see. This must be very pleasant to come home to,' Megan said. 'It's so peaceful.'

The sound of a door slamming was heard and Mrs Jenkins cocked her head. 'And that's him home now, if I'm not mistaken. I'll just go and tell him you're here.'

When she had gone Megan looked round the room. It was pleasantly furnished with a plain brown carpet and chintz covered chairs. A bookcase held a selection of mainly novels and travel books and a delightful old Welsh dresser displayed a collection of antique plates. She was just examining these when the door opened and David Lattimer walked in, a welcoming smile on his face.

'Nice to see you again, Megan. Sorry I was out when you arrived. One of the occupational hazards of a G.P.'s life, I'm afraid.' He went across to the dresser and opened one of the cupboards. 'What can I offer you to drink?'

She smiled. 'A sherry would be nice. And please don't worry about being out. I hope it wasn't anything serious?'

'Child running a high temperature,' he told her briefly. 'Nothing worse than a summer chill as it happens, but better to be safe than sorry.' He handed her a glass. 'Well, how did the first day go?'

'Fine. I really enjoyed it,' she told him. 'At first I felt rather nervous about working on my own but I soon forgot about that. I've always been used to yelling for help if I needed it, you see.'

He smiled. 'I'm sure you're very capable, but if ever you do need any help and I can give it you have only to ask.'

He nodded towards the open window. 'Would you like to see old Matty's garden now?' he asked.

The garden was a joy and they spent some time wandering round it while Megan tried to identify the old-fashioned flowers and plants growing there. It was surrounded by a high wall built of mellow brick and the crowning touch was a gnarled old lilac tree in profuse and fragrant bloom. On the topmost branch a blackbird launched his song onto the still air.

'That must be the most beautiful sound in the world,' Megan said with a sigh.

David nodded. 'It's as though he's reluctant to let the day die.'

Megan glanced at her watch and gave a gasp of surprise when she saw that it was almost nine-thirty. 'Heavens! I'd no idea,' she exclaimed. 'I hope I'm not keeping you from your supper.'

He laughed. 'No. I ate earlier. Mrs Jenkins doesn't live in, you see. She has her own home to attend to and a bachelor son who works in Kingscroft.'

As they walked back into the living room he closed and secured the windows. 'I'd like it if you'd come out to dinner with me one evening, Megan,' he said.

She turned to look at him. 'I'm sure there are other girls who have more claim to your valuable free time than I have,' she said. 'I can't monopolise you, David.'

He looked at her curiously, uncertain how to take her remark. 'Are you asking if I have a regular girl friend, Megan?' he asked bluntly. 'If you are, the answer's no.'

She blushed. Damn! Why had she phrased it so clumsily? 'I'm sorry if it sounded like that,' she said. 'I didn't mean to be nosey. It's just that tongues are quick to wag in small places like this. I wouldn't want to be a source of embarrassment.'

He looked at her calmly, his brown eyes grave. 'I promise you Megan, that the moment I feel in danger of being embarrassed I'll drop you like a hot brick!'

Now it was her turn to be uncertain. She laughed shakily. 'Now I'm afraid you're teasing me, Doctor Lattimer,' she said.

He laughed. 'What a suggestion! I wouldn't dream of it. Come on, if you're ready I'll walk you home.'

As they walked along the wide village

street he took her arm comfortably. 'What about you, Megan? You haven't told me yet whether or not *your* heart is intact.'

She glanced up at him sideways, still unsure of his seriousness. 'Perfectly intact so far,' she said. 'Somehow I've always had too many family commitments until recently. My social life has been practically nil.'

He shook his head. 'That's a sorry state of affairs. I hope we'll be able to put it right.'

'And you – there's been no one special in your life?' She glanced again at his profile in the fading light.

His brow clouded for a moment. 'Maybe once – but that's over. It – I made a mistake. We're none of us immune to those,' he said wistfully.

She said nothing, but for her that one remark clinched her suspicions. At the gate of Celia's cottage she looked up at him.

'Are you coming in for a coffee or a nightcap?'

He shook his head regretfully. 'Better not. I've a mountain of paperwork to get through before I turn in. I'm without a receptionist at the moment. What about Friday then?'

She frowned. 'Friday?'

'For that dinner,' he explained. 'I know a nice little country club.'

'All right. I'd like to.' She smiled.

'Fine. I'll pick you up at eight.' He squeezed her hand. 'Thanks for coming tonight, Megan. I've enjoyed your company. You may not believe this but I'm rather a lonely person.' To her surprise he bent his head and kissed her briefly on the lips, cupping her chin with his hand. 'See you on Friday then,' he said softly. And a moment later he was gone, walking quickly away into the dusk.

As she let herself into the cottage it was quiet and she found Celia busy in the kitchen, writing a long letter to Steve, her fiancé. She glanced up as Megan came in.

'Hello. I didn't expect you yet. There was nothing on T.V so I thought I'd write to Steve.' She spread out a sheet of paper with a list of place names and dates. 'This is the posting schedule. Just look at these dates. It's either weeks between ports or they're calling in each day. It makes letter writing a headache, but I like him to get one from me at every port. Sometimes I run out of news.'

Megan looked over her shoulder at the romantic places on the list and sighed wistfully. 'Lucky Steve. I'd give anything to visit some of those places.'

'And I'd give anything to have him permanently at home,' Celia said. 'Conducting a romance by post is far from satisfactory!'

Megan straightened up. 'I can imagine. Perhaps he'll give it up when you're married. I'll leave you to finish your letter in peace and have that early night, I think,' she said.

As she lay relaxed in bed the last notes of the blackbird's song came through the open window, setting her thinking again about David Lattimer and the conversation they had had.

'Maybe once' he had said in answer to her question about falling in love. 'I made a mistake – we're none of us immune to those.' There was little doubt that he was the man who had let Caroline down so badly. There was something else too; the odd remark he had made, half in jest; 'I promise you that the moment I feel in danger of being embarrassed I'll drop you like a hot brick!' Was that a principle of his? she wondered, the quick, sharp cut, clinical as the surgeon's knife? Well, she'd show him what it felt like to be on the receiving end – without the benefit of an anaesthetic!

She turned over and punched the pillow. 'Right, Doctor Lattimer,' she murmured. 'You may not know it, but the battle's on!'

Hardly before she could turn round

Wednesday afternoon had come again and it was time for her first clinic at Kingscroft Cottage Hospital. As there was nothing booked for Wednesday mornings she had decided to keep them free for her paperwork sessions but, this week, not having worked a full seven days yet, there was not much to do. When she had finished writing reports on the patients she had seen she made herself a sandwich and a cup of coffee and carried them out into the garden.

As she drove into the hospital car park an hour later, she saw that Jeff Maitland's red sports car was already in its place. She smiled to herself. He must have come early especially to beat her to it! She soon found another space, a small one right at the end of a row close to the wall, and backed into it, grateful for the Mini's compactness. In the office she found the coffee percolator bubbling away and as soon as she opened the door she heard Jeff Maitland's laugh ring out. He was teasing one of the office juniors about her new hairstyle. When he saw Megan he bowed exaggeratedly.

'Ah – good afternoon, Miss Lacey. I hope you managed to find a parking space?'

She put her case down on Celia's desk and regarded him coolly. 'Yes, thank you,' she said. Celia offered her a cup of coffee but she shook her head. 'No thanks, I think I'll go straight in and study my notes until the first patient arrives.' And with that she withdrew, conscious of Jeff Maitland's amused glance and the fact that he was waiting till she had closed the door to make some scathing remark about her. She had scarcely had time to settle herself at her desk, however, when the door opened and he breezed in with his accustomed lack of ceremony.

'Is it just that you're dead keen or did I say something to offend you?' he asked bluntly.

She looked up. 'Offend me, Mr Maitland? How could you possibly do that?'

He missed the subtle irony of her remark and grinned, perching himself on the corner of her desk. 'Good. I can't stand touchy women. Actually I wanted to ask you something. How's your schedule? Have you any free time?'

'Well – Wednesday mornings,' she said hesitantly. 'But I'd already set it aside for writing reports–'

'Great!' He slapped his knee. 'For months I've been trying to organise a combined clinic at Brinkdown General and now that we have a speech therapist the team will be complete. Wednesday mornings would suit us both fine!'

She raised an eyebrow. 'Us?'

'Mmm, Maurice Dobbs, the neurologist, and me. Make a note of it, will you? I'll let you know when the details have been finalised.' He got up and made to leave but Megan rose too.

'Just a minute, Mr Maitland,' she said firmly. 'I wish you had told me in the first place what you had in mind. It's true that my Wednesday mornings are free, but it would be extremely inconvenient for me to be at Brinkdown in the mornings and here in the afternoons.' She consulted her timetable. 'Monday mornings would suit me better. I could reshuffle–'

'Out of the question,' he said with a wave of his hand. 'Maurice Dobbs operates on Monday mornings.'

She shook her head. 'I see. Well I'm afraid it will have to be fitted in when I'm in Brinkdown. I have to watch my travel expenses. I can't expect–'

'Oh good God, woman! Don't be so damned penny pinching!' he exploded. 'I'll pay for your petrol myself if that's all that's worrying you. This is important!' He put his palms on her desk and bent to look into her eyes. 'Look, have a think about it and I'll take you out to a meal on Friday evening to discuss it, eh?'

She felt her colour rise angrily. His brashness quite took her breath away. 'It's very *kind* of you, Mr Maitland, but I'm afraid that won't be possible,' she said icily.

He frowned. 'Why?'

'Because I already have a date.'

'Then break it!'

Her mouth dropped open. 'I can't!'

'Why on earth not? Who's it with?'

She drew in her breath sharply. 'Really, Mr Maitland. I think my free time is my own business.'

Just for a second he looked taken aback. 'Oh – all right then – we'll make it tonight instead.' She opened her mouth to protest but he reached out a large hand and ruffled her smooth hair. 'You should get it permed – one of those curly styles. It'd make you look less like a school marm,' he said with a grin and before she had time to make a retort he was gone, slamming the door after him with a characteristic bang.

Grabbing her handbag, Megan found a comb and was just dragging it through her hair when a nurse popped her head round the door.

'Are you ready for the first patient, Miss

Lacey?' Then, seeing Megan's confused state and hasty attempts at tidying herself up, she bit her lip in an attempt not to smile. 'Mr Maitland's awful but it's only his fun. You mustn't take too much notice of him,' she said coyly.

Megan looked back unsmilingly. 'Don't worry. I have no intention of taking any notice of him,' she said through clenched teeth.

It was almost five-thirty when the clinic was over and the last of the patients had gone. Megan picked up her things and went to the office to see if Celia was ready to leave. Only one typist remained, putting the cover on her typewriter and she looked up.

'Celia's already left, but she got your message all right,' the girl said.

'Message?' Megan frowned. 'What message?'

'That you were going out and wouldn't be back for dinner tonight,' the girl told her.

Megan gasped. 'Who said so?' she demanded.

'One of the nurses came in and told her,' came the reply.

'Oh – we'll soon see about that!' Megan muttered under her breath making for the car park. 'If Mr Maitland thinks he can organise my free time as well as my work he's got another think coming!'

But when she reached the place where she had parked the Mini she was in for a shock. Someone had completely blocked her in – and there were no prizes for guessing who! Right across the front of her car stood a red sports car. All that was missing was its owner. Then she saw the note pinned to the windshield by one of the wipers. 'Be with you in a minute,' it read. 'Don't run away!' He hadn't even bothered to sign it!

Fuming, Megan got into the Mini and waited. There was nothing else she could do under the circumstances. When he came back she would tell him exactly what she thought of him. She could hardly wait. Drumming her fingers on the steering wheel she sat there as the minutes ticked by – fifteen, twenty – then she saw him come out of the building. With him was the lovely red-head he had brought to the party, Staff Nurse Simms, and it was only too clear that they were having some sort of disagreement. Finally, the girl flounced off in an obvious huff and Jeff came loping towards her. She drew in a deep breath.

'Mr Maitland,' she began. 'I hope you realise that you've been holding me up for the past twenty minutes!'

He grinned maddeningly. 'Sounds delightful!' He crouched down till his face was on a level with hers at the car window. 'If you just follow me I know a nice pub where they serve good food early in the evening.' He held up his hand as she opened her mouth. 'Please don't argue, Megan. So that you didn't have to break your Friday date I've broken one *I* had for tonight. It's for the sake of our work – nothing else – understand?'

The impish smile had gone from his face and as the piercing blue eyes looked into hers she felt suddenly rather small.

'Yes – yes of course,' she said quietly.

'That's my girl!' The grin was back and a large hand came through the car window to ruffle her hair again. 'Knew you'd see sense if I spoke firmly to you!' He jumped into his own car and switched on the ignition, revving the engine noisily. 'Follow me!' he shouted, roaring out of the car park while Megan was still scrabbling in her bag for a comb.

'Oh!' she gasped, almost in tears with fury. 'Oh you – you despicable man!'

CHAPTER THREE

The Rose and Crown was a tiny pub with a thatched roof and Tudor oak beams and it nestled among trees on the edge of a pretty village about five miles from Kingscroft.

Megan drew up breathlessly behind the red sports car, the rear of which she was rapidly growing to hate. The drive had been nightmarish as she tried desperately to keep up with Jeff. Neither her driving nor her car could match his for speed and she felt hot and agitated as she climbed out of the Mini and locked its doors. Jeff ambled over to her.

'Time you got yourself a decent set of wheels,' he advised. 'That thing looks fit to fall apart!'

'Well, I'm sorry if it doesn't meet with your approval, but it's all I can afford on my salary,' she told him.

'False economy,' he said dogmatically. 'Next thing you know you'll find yourself stranded miles from anywhere in the middle of the night, then what'll you do?'

61

'I can look after myself, thank you!' She glanced at the car. 'It's serviced regularly and hasn't let me down yet. A car doesn't have to roar along the road like a meteor to be efficient, you know.'

'All right!' He spread his hands. 'But don't say I didn't warn you.'

'I shall try to restrain myself from saying that, Mr Maitland,' she said wryly.

He pushed a hand through the thatch of fair hair and regarded her. 'When are you going to stop being so formal? Maitland is fine during working hours, but surely now you can get that stiff little upper lip of yours round the name Jeff!'

Inside the Rose and Crown it was cool and dim, the late sunshine glinting on the copperware that decorated the walls. They took their drinks over to the inglenook fireplace and after a while, ordered chicken salad with French bread, followed by Black Forest gateau. Sipping her sherry, Megan began to relax and as Jeff unfolded his plan for the combined clinic she found her interest aroused. She had been involved in a similar scheme in her previous job and was able to tell him of some of the results achieved. He was enthusiastic.

'I shall certainly keep pressing for it,' he

said. 'And don't worry too much about your car expenses. That's a minor detail.' He looked at her. 'Do you like it here, Megan? Have you made any friends yet? I know quite a lot of people. I could take you out and introduce you around if you like.'

Once more she felt irritation at his brashness. 'Don't worry yourself about me,' she said with more than a hint of acid in her voice. 'I've made as many friends as I have time for at the moment.'

He thrust out his lower lip. 'Is that another way of telling me to mind my own business?' He leaned forward, his eyes twinkling in the way that she was beginning to recognise. 'Ah yes, you have a date for Friday, haven't you? Now, don't tell me, let me guess – you've joined the local sewing circle. Or is it the ladies' choir?'

'Wrong both times!' Immediately she was annoyed with herself for rising to the bait so easily. She took a deep breath, straightening her back. 'But I don't think you need concern yourself with what I do in my own time, do you?'

His eyes narrowed and darkened as he looked at her. 'Back home in Melbourne I've got a sister who gets on her high horse just the way you do,' he said quietly. 'Do you know what I do about it?'

Megan shrugged. 'I can't imagine.'

'I put her across my knee and give her a good hard whacking!' The corners of his mouth twitched. 'So you'd better watch the way you talk to me!'

She felt her cheeks burn as she drank the last of her coffee and looked at her watch. 'I'd better be going. I didn't realise how late it was. Thank you for the meal – Jeff.' She stood up and collected her bag and coat. He followed her out to the car park and watched her unlock the Mini in silence.

'I hope you enjoy yourself on Friday,' he said as she settled herself in the driving seat.

'I expect to, thank you,' she said, looking in her bag for the ignition key.

'Tell me – do you always get what you expect?' he asked.

She turned to look at him. 'It depends what it is,' she said coolly. 'Sometimes it's necessary to avoid it!' And with a twist of the key she brought the Mini's engine to life. She put the car into gear and was about to move off when he bent down to the window.

'I'm playing cricket for the hospital eleven on Sunday,' he told her. 'It's us versus the Grammar School staff. Come and watch – bring Celia if you like. I've a feeling she needs cheering up.' And before she had time to consent or refuse he walked away to his own car with a casual wave of the hand.

Friday evening was warm and mellow as she dressed for her dinner date with David and Megan found herself in a light-hearted mood. Her first week was over and she felt she had done well. The weekend lay ahead of her. Everything seemed to be going according to plan. She thought of Jeff Maitland's words: 'Do you always get what you expect?' Generally she did, because that was the way she arranged her life. To get the best out of things one had to be organised. It was the only way. But she had to confess that she was unsure of David Lattimer. For a man who had cruelly jilted a vulnerable girl, he seemed so nice, so genuinely caring. Of course, it could be a facade – what was the old-fashioned term? – a 'bedside manner' especially cultivated. Only time would tell.

She regarded herself critically in the mirror. She had chosen a cream silk two-piece to wear this evening, with an emerald green scarf at the neck and her newly shampooed hair shone like a polished chestnut. Celia put her head round the door and whistled her approval.

'You'll make a very handsome couple,' she said with a hint of wistfulness in her voice. 'I was just thinking how pleasant it would be to be going out for the evening with a handsome man.'

Megan turned to look at her. It couldn't be much fun, having a fiancé whom one hardly saw. Suddenly she remembered Jeff Maitland's invitation.

'How would you like to go to a cricket match on Sunday?' she asked. 'Jeff Maitland told me he was playing for the hospital and to come and bring you too if you were doing nothing else. I believe it's on the Grammar School playing field.'

Celia's face brightened. 'That might be fun. I did half promise to go and visit an old aunt of mine on Sunday evening, but I could go on there after the match.'

'Fine. That's a date then.' Megan smiled.

A ring at the doorbell downstairs sent Celia to answer it and Megan to take a last look into the mirror.

David's car was certainly more comfortable than the Mini and Megan enjoyed the drive out to the country club. The 'Melrose' was a converted stately home, furnished with discreet good taste, just the sort of place that Megan would have imagined David liking. They had a drink in the bar, then went into the dining room where the lights were low and the food and wine excellent. After they had eaten they took their coffee in the lounge where romantic piped music played, quietly enough not to interfere with conversation.

Megan sat back in the relaxed atmosphere and looked around her appreciatively. 'This is very nice. Do you often come here?'

David smiled. 'When I have someone special to entertain. I thought you'd like it. It's so restful. A lot of places nowadays make you feel exhausted as soon as you walk in through the door!'

Megan wondered whether he had been in the habit of bringing Caroline here. 'I hope this place doesn't bring back unhappy memories for you,' she said.

He looked at her curiously, then smiled. 'I don't know why you should think that, but if it did I would have laid their ghosts well and truly by bringing you here.'

She blushed. 'That's a very pretty compliment.'

He wanted to know all about her week's work and she found herself talking far more than she had intended to. The evening went swiftly and she was disappointed to find that they were on their way home before she had had the chance to find out any more about David's past. In any case, he seemed determined not to talk about himself. The more she saw of him the more she liked him and she had to admit that it was growing more and more difficult to believe him the type of man who could let anyone down.

As they drew up outside the cottage he turned to her, his eyes gentle in the soft light.

'Thank you for coming out with me this evening, Megan. I've enjoyed myself very much,' he said. 'I hope we can perhaps make our relationship more permanent – I mean, that you'll let me take you out regularly.' His hand reached out and covered hers. 'Forgive me. I'm not usually so inarticulate. It's the effect you have on me. Can you understand that?'

She tried to laugh without much success. 'Why don't you come in for a last coffee?' she said. Suddenly she wanted to be where the lights were brighter, where there was company. She had wanted him to be attracted to her but now she wasn't sure if she could handle the situation. To her surprise he agreed and they got out of the car. But inside the cottage Megan found that Celia had left a note, saying that she had gone into Brinkdown to the cinema.

She left David in the living room while she made coffee, busying herself unnecessarily round the kitchen, wondering what to do and say next. When at last she carried the tray through she found that he had put a record on. It was one of her favourite Schubert quartets, and she sat down to listen, grateful for the excuse not to talk. They drank their coffee in silence until the record ended, then he said:

'You didn't answer my question, Megan. Will you come out with me again?'

She smiled. 'Of course – I'd love to. Celia and I are going to a cricket match on Sunday. It's the hospital versus the Grammar School staff. Why don't you come with us?'

But he shook his head. 'I can't. I'm on duty this weekend.'

He reached out and took her hand. 'I'm not very good at speeches, Megan, but I'm trying to say that I like you very much. More than that – I – find you very attractive. Oh damn!' He stood up and walked to the fireplace where he turned and looked at her. 'What I'm attempting to say is that I think I may be falling in love with you. Do you find that horrifying?'

She shook her head slowly. 'Of course I don't, David. Why should I?'

He shrugged. 'I just wanted you to know what to expect, that's all. It's only fair. Now you can tell me to leave if you want to.'

She stood up and went towards him. Why was he suddenly so jumpy and insecure? 'Please don't say that,' she said. 'I wouldn't dream of telling you to leave. Do you feel like this because of the – the mistake you told me you once made?'

He nodded. 'I suppose so. An experience like that shakes one's confidence.' He smiled. 'You're a very sweet, understanding person, Megan. I'm sure you could help me to put the past firmly behind me.'

She put her hands on his shoulders. 'I'd like to think that I could do that.'

He put out his arms and drew her towards him, burying his face in her hair, then his lips found hers in a light kiss. She felt her heart contract. Could she go through with it, this deception? Could she really take revenge on someone who seemed so vulnerable himself? She closed her eyes as David kissed her again, then she heard a sound and opened them. Celia stood in the doorway and David sprang guiltily from her.

'I must go,' he said, looking at his watch. 'I'll ring you, Megan. Goodnight.'

'Goodnight, David – and thank you for a lovely evening,' she said as he hurried from the room. She smiled at Celia. 'What a shy man he is.'

Celia nodded. 'Yes, isn't he?'

The following day, Saturday, the girls cleaned the cottage from top to bottom, then they went into Kingscroft in Megan's Mini for the shopping. As they drove Celia held her head on one side, a frown creasing her brow.

'There's an odd noise,' she said. 'Your engine doesn't sound quite right to me, Megan.'

Megan laughed. 'It never has! This car has a character all of its own. It doesn't sound like other cars. You're used to your lovely new Fiesta, so naturally this one would sound odd to you.'

They collected the week's food from the supermarket and went home to relax in the garden for the rest of the afternoon. Megan had half expected David to ring and ask her out, but she remembered that he had said he was on call, so she washed her hair and did her laundry instead. As the girls sat together in the evening she suddenly asked:

'How do you know when you're in love?'

Celia laughed. 'I should say when you don't have to ask *that* question. Why?'

Megan shrugged. 'It's only just occurred to me that I never have been. Most girls of my age have probably been in love half a dozen times, but somehow I've always been too taken up with other people's problems to get round to it.'

Celia put her head on one side. 'And now you think you may be. Is that it?'

'Let's say that for the first time I'm considering the possibility,' Megan hedged. 'It's David Lattimer who thinks he may be, though of course that's strictly between ourselves.'

Celia's eyes widened. 'I see. Well, I suppose I should have read the signs clearly enough last night.'

'He seems to have had an unhappy love affair some time in the past,' Megan told her. Do you know anything about it?'

'Won't he tell you himself?'

Megan shook her head. 'Only that he made a mistake.'

'Well, I should leave it at that if I were you,' Celia advised. 'Sometimes it's better to let sleeping dogs lie. If you really think you love him you could be the happy ending he's looking for.' She took up her sewing and Megan watched her, deep in her own thoughts. She wasn't at all sure now that she was the kind of person who enjoyed revenge. Just what *was* the truth about Caroline's affair with David? If only she knew.

Sunday dawned brilliantly. When the girls got up the sun was already a fierce yellow ball of heat and the sky was a bright tropical blue.

'A wonderful day for the match,' Megan observed as they ate breakfast.

Celia looked out of the window at the sky. 'Too good to last. This hot weather has gone on for a long time now. We're about due for a thunderstorm, I'd say.'

Megan laughed. 'You're cheerful! I'm sure it won't rain today.'

'Well, I shall take an umbrella just in case,' the other girl said cautiously.

Megan's thoughts had been with Caroline over the last twenty-four hours. It was some time since she had had a letter from her, so she decided to ring her this morning at her friend's home. The telephone rang for so long that she thought they must be out, but just as she was about to give up there was a click and the familiar voice of their mother's old friend, Hester, who told Megan that

Caroline was out.

'She has a new job as a "supply" teacher,' Hester told her. 'That will be why you haven't heard from her. She's been very busy.'

'Is she happy?' Megan asked.

'Oh, very,' Hester assured her. 'Since she's been up here she seems a different girl. She loves it in the Highlands. I wouldn't be at all surprised if she decided to stay here permanently.'

Megan tried to feel heartened by the news, but an odd feeling of depression engulfed her for the rest of the morning. There was no denying that the feeling that Caroline could get along better without her hurt. Still, she refused to let Celia see that she was depressed and threw herself wholeheartedly into making the picnic tea for the afternoon. Celia asked if she would like to go along with her afterwards to her aunt's, but she shook her head.

'I think I'd better keep abreast of the paperwork in case this combined clinic comes up,' she said. 'I'll take my own car and come straight home after the match.'

They set out at half past one, in plenty of time for the match which was due to start at two-thirty. It was oppressively hot by now and both girls wore thin cotton dresses and sandals. The ground was packed with members of staff, both from the school and the hospital, while in the little pavilion a band of willing ladies were serving tea and lemonade, cucumber sandwiches and cake.

Megan and Celia sat on the grass with some of the nurses from the hospital, enjoying the sunshine and the leisurely play, drowsing in the afternoon heat as bat hit ball with hypnotic regularity and softly shod feet ran over the grass. Gentle applause came from the select group in front of the pavilion then Jeff Maitland went in to bat – and suddenly everything was changed. Every ball seemed to disappear into space like a guided missile, sending fielders scattering in all directions. There were shouts of 'boundary' again and again and the score on the board went up alarmingly until Jeff was dramatically caught out by the Grammar School games master in a catch that sent him rolling over and over on the grass, the ball clutched to his chest. No one was dozing by the time a perspiring Jeff returned to the pavilion and the applause was more the kind a pop star might expect. Jeff acknowledged it with a wave and a grin, winking at the nearest pretty girl.

Celia laughed. 'Quite a card, our Jeff.'

'Quite a show-off, you mean!' Megan retorted.

They were unpacking their picnic during the tea interval when Jeff joined them, looking giant-like in his white flannels and shirt.

'Hello, girls, enjoying the match?' He stretched his long length on the grass between them, so confident of his welcome that Megan felt the back of her neck tingle with irritation. He leaned over to look into the basket.

'Wow – paté and salad. My favourite!'

Celia laughed. 'Can we press you to join us?'

'I thought you'd never ask!' He reached into the basket and helped himself generously, munching happily as he looked from one girl to the other. 'Well – aren't you going to tell me how well I did? Sixty-four isn't a bad score, is it? Specially as I haven't played since I left home.'

'You certainly made them sit up and take notice,' Celia conceded. 'Though I'm afraid you may have committed the unforgivable sin of making the game exciting!'

He laughed and turned to Megan. 'What do you think? You're very quiet this afternoon.'

'You seemed to be managing very nicely without my admiration and encouragement,' she said. 'I'm afraid we've only brought tea. Is that all right?'

'They've got some cans of cold beer in the pavilion.' He put his hand into his pocket and drew out a handful of loose change. 'Here, hop along and get some for us, eh?' He held the money out to Megan who ignored it, her cheeks burning.

'Tea will do fine for me – thank you,' she said stiffly.

Celia took the money and sat up. 'I'll get them.'

Throwing an arm round her shoulders, Jeff gave her a resounding kiss on the cheek. 'You're a grand girl, Celia. Make that Steve of yours a bonza wife!'

Megan winced at the expression, which she guessed was aimed at annoying her. When Celia had gone he looked at her for a long moment.

'You know, you should learn to relax more,' he said. 'You're going to look old before your time if you keep on frowning like that!'

She shrugged. 'That will be my problem, won't it?'

'I guess so,' he agreed. 'It'd be a pity

though. When you smile you're not bad looking.'

'Thank you,' Megan said crisply. 'You're *very* kind.'

He grinned. 'Not at all. I believe in giving encouragement where it's needed.'

Luckily Celia came back at that moment with the cans of beer and the rest of the meal was eaten in silence by the girls while Jeff regaled them with stories of his cricketing prowess back home in Australia.

'Just you wait till you see me bowl,' he told them. 'I've got a spin like you've never seen before. The second half will be over before you can wink. I'll have the whole lot of them out for a duck!'

And to Megan's annoyance he was almost right. The Grammar School eleven were all out for a very low score, one batsman after another falling to Jeff's demon bowling. As the match drew to a close the girls got to their feet and began to pack the picnic things into the basket. Celia looked at the sky shaking her head.

'A good thing it's over early if you ask me,' she said. 'Just look at that sky. We're in for a storm.' She looked at Megan. 'Shall I take the basket or will you?'

'I'll take it,' Megan offered. 'Then I can

wash the things and put them away. You get off to your aunt's.'

The first drops of rain had begun to fall as they reached the car park and Megan wound up the window and switched on the windscreen wipers.

'Maybe this will clear the air,' she said to herself as she nosed the car out of the car park. The day certainly had been uncomfortably hot and oppressive. As she left the town behind and the country spread out before her the rain began to lash against the windscreen, making it hard to see. She slowed down, wondering whether to stop, then she heard the first rolls of thunder in the distance and decided to press on. If there was one thing she hated, it was being out in a thunderstorm.

She had come to the steep hill halfway between Kingscroft and Little Avedon when the Mini began to cough and splutter. She pressed her foot down hard on the accelerator but there seemed to be no power in the engine at all. She reached the top of the hill with difficulty and pulled over to the side of the road. Already she could see smoke coming out from under the bonnet and she groaned, wishing she'd followed Celia's example and at least brought an umbrella.

She sat for a while, waiting for the rain to let up, but it showed no signs of doing so and, at last, in sheer desperation she got out of the car and opened the bonnet.

Almost immediately she was drenched, the rain, heavy and cold, soaked through the thin material of her dress as though it were blotting paper. Hopelessly, she stared at the mystery under the bonnet, praying for something obvious to present itself. But it all looked the same as ever to her. Smoke still curled up from its depths and the radiator was too hot to touch but what was causing the trouble remained a complete mystery.

What on earth was she to do? She looked around. She was miles from anywhere. There were no houses in sight, no telephone, not even another car she could flag down. There was nothing else for it – she would have to walk the rest of the way home and phone to a garage from there.

Locking the doors securely, she set out, her hair plastered to her head and her teeth chattering. It was like walking under a cold shower and, what was more, she estimated that she had all of three miles to walk in it!

She had gone about half a mile when a sound made her lift her head and listen. A car was coming, she could hear its engine above the splash of the rain. Praying that she could make it stop she stood back, her eyes raking the road, waiting for it to appear. But when it did come it was going so fast that she doubted whether the driver would see her in time.

Desperate, she ran into the middle of the road, waving her arms frantically. The car swerved, slowed and came to a halt some yards further up the road. Her heart lifting, she ran towards it, then her feet faltered. There was something familiar about the shape and colour of the car. It was red with a black canvas top, put up against the weather. Surely she hadn't flagged down Jeff Maitland?

He reversed to where she was standing and wound down the window. 'That's a pretty good way to get yourself killed. Come on – what are you waiting for? Do you want a lift or don't you–' He broke off as recognition dawned. 'My God! Megan! What's happened to you, for heaven's sake?'

'What does it look like?' she said bitterly, very close to tears. 'My car's broken down. Celia's gone to visit an aunt in Brinkdown and I'm walking home.'

'Didn't I tell you that darned thing would let you down?' He reached into the back of the car for a rug which he thrust at her. 'Look, head over there–' he pointed. 'Just through that hedge there's an old barn. I've got some dry things in my bag. You can change.' He reached for his cricket bag and got out of the car.

Megan huddled in the rug, her teeth chattering. 'It's all right, I'm wet through. I might as well wait till I get home.'

'Do as you're told,' he demanded. 'Do you want me to get as wet as you are, standing here arguing?'

The barn was on the other side of the hedge, partially obscured by trees. Jeff was close behind her, carrying the cricket bag, a ground sheet draped around his shoulders. In the barn he opened the bag and brought out a towel.

'Take off your things and dry yourself on this,' he said. 'It is a clean one. As it happens I brought two this afternoon.' She stared at him and he pushed a hand through his hair in exasperation. 'Oh, for heaven's sake, I won't look! And anyway, I haven't been a doctor all this time without seeing a few bodies. It's no novelty to me!' He delved into the bag again and brought out a large cricket sweater. 'I reckon this will more than cover you,' he said throwing it at her. 'Can't do much about the feet though. I guess I'll have to carry you back to the car.'

He turned his back and she peeled off her wet dress, drying herself gratefully on the thick towel, then she pulled the sweater over her head. It came right down to her knees, its sleeves flopping over her hands. She felt ridiculous as she rolled them up in an effort to look better.

'Are you decent yet?' He turned round and immediately burst into gales of laughter. 'Oh my God, Megan! What a sketch you look!'

She felt helpless tears prick at her eyelids. 'You don't have to tell me that,' she said. 'You really are an insensitive brute, aren't you? I – I hate you!'

He stopped laughing abruptly and came towards her. 'That's not a very nice thing to say to me when I've just rescued you from a watery grave!' He took the towel out of her hand. 'Here, you haven't dried your hair, it's still dripping.' He rubbed at her hair till she thought her teeth would rattle. 'Actually,' he said, 'you look rather sweet. Like a little girl dressed up in the grown-ups' clothes. There, I think that'll do.' He threw the towel into the bag and turned back to her. 'Are you cold?' Without warning he pulled her to him and kissed her. She gasped, stiff in his arms, but the feel of his lips on hers took her breath away.

He held her a little away from him and shook her gently. 'Relax, Megan. You're a woman, not a block of ice!' His voice was low and husky and as he spoke something inside her seemed to melt. As his arms went round her again she leaned against him, then her arms crept round his neck and when his lips found hers again she responded as she had never known she could. Her head spun crazily and she felt as though she couldn't breathe. He held her close for a moment, then hoisted her into his arms as though she weighed nothing.

'Come on, better get you home and back to normal,' he said.

But Megan felt as though nothing would ever be quite normal again.

CHAPTER FOUR

It was half past eight when Celia returned to the cottage and she was surprised to find Megan sitting in the darkening living room, apparently staring into space. She switched on the table lamp, looking at her friend with concern.

'Are you all right, Megan? I would have been back earlier but I stayed till the storm was over. Was it bad here?'

Megan blinked, dragging her thoughts together. 'What? Oh, the weather – yes it's been awful. My car broke down on the way home and I thought I'd have to walk the last three miles.'

'Oh no! And you didn't even have a mac,' Celia exclaimed. 'What did you do?'

'I flagged a car down – and it turned out to be Jeff Maitland of all people. He brought me home.'

Celia smiled. 'He's really very good-hearted under all that bluff. But what about your car? Where is it now?'

'The car? Oh, he said he'd go back and

have a look at it,' Megan said, still rather dazedly.

Celia went into the kitchen only to reappear a moment later holding Jeff's sweater. 'What's this?'

Megan looked up. 'It's Jeff's. I was so wet that he insisted I change into it. There was this old barn, you see–' She trailed off as Celia burst out laughing.

'I'd like to have been there. You must have looked a dish in this!'

Suddenly Megan joined in her laughter. 'I did. It gave Jeff a big laugh and I was furious with him at the time. But I can see the funny side of it now.' The telephone bell cut through their laughter and Megan jumped up to answer it. 'That may be him now, reporting on the state of the Mini.'

It was, but the news wasn't good. 'I'm afraid it looks like a big job, Megan,' he said. 'But I told them that your car is essential to your work and they've agreed to lend you one till yours is fixed.'

'Oh, thank you, Jeff,' she said. 'It's very good of you to take the trouble.'

'Are you all right?' he asked.

'Perfectly, thank you.'

'Good. I'll go then. Someone will deliver the car to you on Monday morning. Bye.'

'Goodbye – and thanks again.' As she hung up she was seeing his face above hers again, his eyes momentarily soft; feeling his strong hands on her shoulders, his lips, warm and firm on hers.

'Was that about the car?'

She jerked her mind back to the present as she realised that Celia was talking to her. 'Oh – er – yes. The garage is going to lend me one. It looks as though mine will be in dock for some time.'

'Oh, what bad luck. Are you worried about it?'

'Worried?' Megan looked at her.

'Well, you looked so pensive,' Celia explained. 'So – preoccupied. I thought maybe it was money.'

Megan laughed. 'I see what you mean. No, I'm not that hard up, though I realise now that the Mini was a bad investment. I'm just a bit tired, that's all. Shall we have supper now? I'll feel better when I've eaten.'

The week that followed sped past. On the Monday Megan had a phone call from David asking her to dine with him on Thursday. She had hoped to be able to thank Jeff in person when she saw him at the Wednesday afternoon clinic, but he was in London attending a conference that day, and his clinic was taken by another doctor. She found herself absurdly disappointed. For some reason she desperately wanted him to know that she could laugh at herself. How stuffy she must have appeared to him till now.

On Thursday morning she was delighted to see Peter Forbes making real headway on his second visit to the clinic at Brinkdown Health Centre. He had been the week before and had met some of the other patients, including a young man of about his own age who was recovering from a similar accident. The two had taken to each other on sight and Megan could see that from now on it would be a matter of competition between the two of them. Both boys could read perfectly well and Peter could write, though John Marshall's hands were still too badly damaged. Megan began the laborious business of teaching Peter to articulate properly again. He was impatient and still inclined to become frustrated, but by the end of the session his mother was delighted with the progress they had made. She had found out something else, too. Chatting to John's mother she discovered that the two women had been at school together.

'In that case maybe the four of you could get together,' she suggested. 'I'm sure it would help the boys. I understand that they have interests in common. Why not play the game we play here of putting a number of small objects on a tray and getting them to name them one by one?'

Mrs Forbes grew quite excited. 'They could have a race!' she said enthusiastically.

'As long as they're not in too much of a hurry,' Megan reminded her. 'Better to go slowly and get it right.'

As she drove home that evening Megan wondered how long her own car would be. The one the garage had lent her was larger than she was used to and besides using more petrol it was harder to drive and park. When she let herself into the cottage she was surprised that no smell of cooking came from the kitchen. She was going out to dinner herself, but she had left a meat pie in the fridge for Celia. On the hall table was a letter addressed to her. It bore a Scottish post mark and she tore it open eagerly. Caroline certainly seemed to be busy, just as Hester had said. She was enjoying meeting many new people in her job as supply teacher and she had joined the local tennis club and amateur dramatics. Megan folded the somewhat brief letter and pushed it back into its envelope thoughtfully. Was Caroline putting on a brave show for her benefit? She wished she could go up to Scotland and see for herself, but she wouldn't get a holiday at all now this year. Anyway, at least the girl was keeping herself busy and that would help to heal the ache, she was sure.

She pushed open the kitchen door and stopped short as she saw Celia sitting at the table staring at an official looking letter spread out before her.

'Haven't you put your meal on?' she asked. 'Shall I light the oven?'

But Celia shook her head despondently. 'I'm not very hungry thanks.' She looked up and Megan saw to her concern that she had been crying.

'Celia! What is it, love? It's not Steve?'

The other girl shook her head. 'No – though I wish he were here right now. I badly need someone's advice. It's this letter. It's from Gran's solicitor. It appears that when Grandad died she borrowed a sum of money from a close friend to pay off what was still owing on this cottage. He never pressed for repayment, but now he has died himself and his relatives are demanding the money back as soon as possible.' Her eyes filled with tears. 'It looks as though I may have to sell the cottage after all, Megan.'

'Oh, Celia, surely not. Is there no other way?' Megan sat down opposite her at the table.

'If there is I can't see it.' Celia shook her head. 'The best thing for me to do is to make an appointment with the solicitor as soon as I can and find out exactly where I stand.' She looked up. 'I'm sorry, Megan.'

'Sorry? What for?'

'I shall feel I've let you down if I have to sell up,' Celia said tearfully.

Megan patted her shoulder. 'Good heavens, don't worry about me! Look, maybe we could even get a flat together. We could move into Kingscroft and then you'd be nearer your work. What do you say?' But to her horror Celia burst into tears.

'Oh, forgive me – I know you meant it kindly,' she sobbed. 'But the thought of giving up the cottage – of moving away from this village and – and – the people here is more than I can bear. I'd rather give up my job than the cottage any day!'

'Then maybe *that's* the answer,' Megan said. 'At least you wouldn't have the travelling expenses. You could even sell your car. Would that raise enough money to pay off the debt, do you think?'

Celia looked slightly cheered. 'That *is* an

idea. But I have to have a job and where would I find one here?'

The two girls sank once more into gloomy silence until suddenly Megan remembered something that David Lattimer had said to her. 'I think I may have an idea,' she said slowly. 'But I won't raise your hopes till I've made some enquiries. Keep your fingers crossed.' She looked at her watch. 'I'll have to hurry now and get ready or David will be here for me.' As she stood by the door she looked at Celia's slumped shoulders. 'Look, why don't you come with us? I'm sure David wouldn't mind,' she said. 'He's fond of you and if he knew you'd got trouble—'

But Celia shook her head vigorously. 'I wouldn't dream of playing gooseberry! No, I'll be perfectly all right. I feel much better already. You go off and enjoy yourself.' She stood up and began to bustle round the kitchen, making a great show of laying the table and preparing to eat. 'I think I do feel hungry after all now,' she announced with forced brightness.

When he arrived, David told her that he had tickets for a concert at Brinkdown Town Hall and it was as they were driving there that Megan told him about Celia's trouble.

'I seem to remember you telling me that

you were without a receptionist,' she said. 'Are you still?'

He nodded. 'I am and it's getting me down, trying to cope with it all. Mrs Jenkins does her best, taking messages and answering the phone, but as I told you, she doesn't live in and that makes life difficult. Not many efficient receptionists want to bury themselves in a village like this, even the married ones prefer to travel into Kingscroft.'

Megan beamed. 'Then you can consider your troubles over! Celia is looking for a job in the village. She has all the experience you would need and I'm sure she'd jump at the job.'

A curious expression crossed his face. 'Well – I'll certainly offer it to her,' he said guardedly. 'But she may not be as keen as you seem to think. I couldn't offer her as much salary as she's getting now for instance.'

'I don't think that would matter too much,' she told him. 'For a start, she wouldn't have the travelling expenses. She wants to sell the car, you see.' Another idea hit her suddenly and she gave a squeak of excitement. 'Of course! Why didn't I think of it before? *I* could buy her car! I'll have to replace mine anyway!'

David looked at her and laughed. 'This is

certainly your night for ideas, isn't it?'

She could hardly take in the concert. All she wanted was to get home to Celia and cheer her up with the news. She longed to see her friend's face brighten again. They ate in a little Italian restaurant, then drove home. In the car David turned to her with a smile.

'You're like a little girl at Christmas,' he told her. 'The excitement almost makes you glow in the dark!'

'I want you to come in and offer her the job,' she told him. 'She'll never believe me if I tell her.' She looked at him, 'You will, won't you?'

To her surprise he seemed reluctant, but she managed to persuade him and together they went into the cottage and found Celia in the living room, curled up in front of the television with a mug of cocoa.

'David has something to ask you,' Megan announced, trying not to sound too triumphant. She waited, looking from one to the other, puzzled about the tension in the air. Finally David said:

'Megan has been telling me that you want to work here in the village. I'm in need of a receptionist. The job is yours if you want it.'

Celia flushed. 'I – I'd be very pleased to

take it – thank you, David.'

'And I'll buy the car from you – if you'll sell it to me,' Megan put in. 'I mean – you know me, don't you – and you could always have it back again when you're able–' She broke off, getting the feeling that she was talking too much. Celia stood up.

'I think I'll go up to bed now. Goodnight, David – and thanks again.' She closed the door firmly behind her and Megan looked at David.

'She *was* pleased. I'm sure she was. It's just that she's had an awful day, I expect.'

He nodded. 'Of course.'

'I'll make some coffee,' she said. 'Or would you like something stronger?'

He held out his hand to her. 'That can wait. Come and sit down. There's something I want to talk to you about. All evening we've talked about other people. Now I want to talk about you – about us.'

She sat beside him feeling hesitant and nervous and he put an arm round her shoulders, drawing her close.

'What are your plans for the future, Megan?' he asked.

Suddenly the reason for her being here in Little Avedon loomed very large and she cleared her throat. 'I – don't know that I have any – for myself,' she said truthfully.

He kissed the top of her head. 'You're a very sweet, unselfish person, Megan.'

'No – no I'm not,' she said uncomfortably. 'Sometimes I have very unkind thoughts about people.'

He laughed. 'Don't we all? Seriously though – what do you want from life? Where do you go from here?'

She frowned thoughtfully. 'Well, I love my work, but eventually I suppose I want what most girls want – a home, a husband and children.' She laughed. 'It sounds very dull and unliberated, doesn't it?'

He shook his head. 'Not at all. It sounds, well, like you. It's what I thought you'd want. It's nice to be right about someone, especially someone you've come to think of as special.' His arm tightened round her. 'Megan – I know we haven't known each other for very long, but I feel very close to you. The life of a country G.P. isn't easy, but like you, I love my work and can't imagine ever wanting to change it.' He looked down at her. 'How would you feel about sharing it with me?'

She stared at him. Was he really asking her to marry him after such a short time? Was this what happened with Caroline? Was he a creature of impulse?

'I – don't know, David,' she said hesitantly. 'We've known each other such a short time.'

'I don't expect you to answer right away. Of course you'll want time to think about it. Please don't think I'm trying to rush you.' He drew her close and kissed her. 'But it could be a good life, Megan; a very good life. You could carry on with your job if you wanted. Will you give it some serious thought?'

Megan hardly slept at all that night. What had happened was so unexpected. Never in her wildest dreams had she expected David to ask her to marry him and certainly not so soon! Of course it was just the chance she should have welcomed – to keep him on tenterhooks for as long as she chose and then let him down just as he had let Caroline down. But somehow that idea was growing less and less attractive. David was so thoroughly nice – even if she wasn't in love with him she still liked him a lot and, after all, the old saying was right: two wrongs didn't make a right. She tossed and turned. If only she could find out what went wrong between Caroline and him. That would put a totally different complexion on things. Then there was this trouble of Celia's. Would she be able to give her enough money for the car? And why had Celia been so cool about the job David had offered her? Why was nothing straight forward?

At breakfast next morning she saw that Celia hadn't slept well either. She was quiet and there were dark rings under her eyes. Even the airmail letter in the post that obviously came from Steve failed to cheer her up. Megan touched her arm.

'Celia – I hope I didn't put you in an awkward situation last night – about the job, I mean. I'm sure David would understand if you wanted to change your mind about it.'

The other girl looked up sharply. 'Why? Did he say anything about it after I'd gone to bed?'

'No. It's just that you seemed a little, well, reluctant about it,' Megan explained.

Celia sighed. 'I suppose I should have told you. I worked for David once before, almost two years ago. It was when I first came here to look after Gran when her arthritis got bad. It was David who wrote to me to ask me to come. He was her doctor, you see, and he felt she shouldn't be living alone.'

'I see,' said Megan, not really seeing at all. 'And it didn't work out – is that what you're saying?'

Celia lifted her shoulders. 'It wasn't that.

It was fine – ideal, being so close to home. It was Steve. We'd just become engaged at the time. He came home on leave and met David. For some reason he didn't like the idea of us working together, so I had to leave and get the job at Kingscroft Cottage Hospital.'

'And you feel that the situation may still be the same, even after all this time?' Megan said thoughtfully. 'Surely he can trust you by now?'

'Well, I've made up my mind, so if he can't he'll have to do the other thing,' Celia said bitterly. 'I don't like the job he does, but I can't see him giving it up for me! And after all, I do have this debt to pay off.' She looked at Megan and smiled suddenly. 'Don't look so worried, love. You did what you thought would be a help – and it *is*. I'm taking the job and I'm grateful, really I am. It's really good of you to offer to buy the car too. It'll be nice not to lose sight of it altogether. You're a real friend!'

Megan pressed her hand. 'You can have the use of it whenever you want. That goes without saying. Let's get it all fixed up as soon as we can, eh?'

Celia nodded. 'I'm going to make an appointment to see the solicitor this morning. I've a feeling it'll all work out fine after all.'

It was the following Wednesday afternoon, just before the clinic was due to start that Jane Lang, the physiotherapist, dropped in to see Megan.

'How are you getting on?' she asked. 'I haven't seen you to speak to since the party Celia gave for you when you first came.'

Megan looked at her in surprise. Her voice sounded oddly hoarse. 'Have you got a cold?' she asked.

The other girl shook her head. 'My voice, you mean? No. I'm a bit bothered about it actually. It just sort of came on and I think it's getting worse.'

'Is it sore?' Megan asked.

Again Jane shook her head. 'No, that's the funny part. It sounds awful, doesn't it?'

'It certainly doesn't sound too good,' Megan agreed. 'Look, why don't you ask Jeff Maitland to have a look at it?'

'Oh, I'm sure there's no need for that,' Jane said. 'I don't like to bother him. It's a bit of strain, I expect. It'll soon pass.'

'All the same, it would do no harm. Better to be safe than sorry,' Megan warned, 'Especially in your job.'

Jane coloured slightly. 'It can't be a virus or anything I might pass on,' she said defensively. 'If it were I'd have other symptoms like pain and a temperature.' She looked at Megan and lifted her shoulders. 'Oh, all right. I know I should get it looked at really. It's quite true what they say about people in the medical profession being the worst offenders when it comes to neglecting themselves.'

Megan picked up the telephone. 'I'll see if he can see you this afternoon.'

It appeared that Jeff had started his clinic early, but he promised to fit Jane in before he went home.

The afternoon went smoothly. Megan was establishing a good rapport with most of her patients and she found her work absorbing and satisfying. She was just saying goodbye to the last patient when Jeff Maitland came in, his white coat flying open and his hair as unruly as ever.

'What's all this about our Jane then?' he wanted to know. 'Hasn't she got a G.P. of her own?'

As usual he didn't bother to keep his voice down and Megan got up and closed the door pointedly. 'It's just that I don't like the sound of her voice,' she told him. 'I thought you might have a look at her throat – off the record. I've a feeling that if she went to her G.P. he'd refer her to you anyway.'

He sat down in the chair opposite, putting his feet up on the corner of her desk and regarding her with amused eyes.

'Dear me, Doctor! What do you think it can be?' he asked her in a mocking tone.

She ignored it. 'As a matter of fact I think she may be developing a laryngeal web,' she said.

He threw back his head and roared with laughter. 'Oh Megan, you're a caution, you really are! A laryngeal web, eh? Very dramatic!'

'I have *seen* a few cases,' she told him. 'Though I admit that they've all been post-operative. But you don't have to take my word for it, do you?' She looked at him sitting there on the other side of her desk, his long limbs stretched out like a cat's. She looked at his golden skin, the blue eyes and thick, uncontrollable hair; the deep cleft in his chin, and her heart turned a quick somersault. Almost as though he read her thoughts he looked up and smiled.

'Well, I'll have a look at her. Tell you what – wait for me and we'll have a meal together afterwards.'

She felt her cheeks burning. 'Oh – I don't know – I–'

He stood up. 'Surely you want to know whether your diagnosis is correct? I'll pick you up in about twenty minutes.' And without waiting for her reply he whirled out of the room.

She gathered her things together and went to the office to find Celia. Why was it she could never refuse Jeff? True, he never gave her much of a chance to, but she could always get out of it if she really *wanted* to. She closed her mind to the thoughts that tormented her. It was all in the line of duty, she told herself. She did want to know if her diagnosis was correct after all.

She caught Celia just as she was leaving and told her she would be out for dinner, then she went out to the car park to wait for Jeff. She didn't see him come out of the building and when his voice spoke close to her ear she started violently. He laughed.

'You're as jumpy as a kitten, Megan. May I prescribe a good tranquiliser?'

She blushed. 'You shouldn't creep up on people like that.'

He looked at the borrowed car. 'This is a bit of an old heap they've lent you. Have they let you know yet when yours will be ready?'

'As a matter of fact I'm selling it, getting a new one,' she told him.

He grinned. 'Glad to hear you take my advice sometimes. Just follow me, you can tell me all about it later.'

After a short drive his car drew up outside a tall Victorian house and Megan stopped behind him, puzzled. When he got out of his car and came towards her she asked:

'Where's this?'

He grinned. 'My place. Oh, don't worry, I haven't got designs on your virtue, just a large piece of steak I bought yesterday. It's in the fridge right this minute. It'd be a pity to waste it.'

She got out of the car with as much dignity as she could manage. Why was it that he always made her look and feel so stuffy? 'That's fine with me,' she said lightly. 'As long as you're not expecting me to cook it for you. That would be the end!'

He narrowed his eyes at her. 'I'll settle for some help. Share the food, share the chores – okay?'

Inside, the flat was spacious and furnished just as Megan would have expected, in a rather spartan way. There were plenty of photographs around, mainly of cricket and football teams. There were some earlier groups taken at college too and some that were obviously of his family. The kitchen was surprisingly organised, with everything neatly in its place. Megan remarked on it.

'If there's one thing I can't stand,' he said getting lettuce and tomatoes out of the fridge, 'it's a messy kitchen. I like my food and I'm particular about the way it's prepared.'

The steak that he took out made Megan's eyes pop. It must have weighed at least a pound and a half. 'I see what you mean about its being a pity to waste it,' she remarked. 'Don't give me too much. I'm not used to it.' She watched him season it expertly and put it under the grill. 'Shall I make the salad?' she asked. He nodded.

'Great. By the way, I hate to admit it, but you were probably right about Jane. I shall have to do some more investigation, of course, but I think it is a web.'

She bit her lip. 'Poor Jane. You'll operate?'

He lifted his shoulders, 'What else? It will have to be removed. That'll mean a job for you afterwards.'

She nodded. 'I suppose it could have been worse.'

He grinned at her. 'So – clever Megan, eh? Now, how about some music? Why don't you go through and put on a record? You'll find them in the cupboard under the record player.'

In the living room she pulled out a few of the records and studied their jackets, wondering what his taste in music would be. The first one she found was a selection of Rugby songs and she thrust it back hurriedly, the next was Beethoven's fifth symphony. She smiled. Yes, he would like its robustness. She put it on the turntable and turned up the volume so that he would hear it in the kitchen. As the first notes filled the room he put his head round the door.

'The Victory symphony, eh? Very appropriate in view of your correct diagnosis!' He put the plates of steak onto the table and reappeared a moment later with the bowl of salad.

When they had reached the coffee stage Jeff took the record off and replaced it with a soft, romantic one, then he held his hand out to Megan.

'I think this one is better for the digestion. Come and sit down. You know you really should try to relax. Are you always this tense or is it just the effect that I have on you?'

'Why should you imagine that *you* make me feel tense?' she asked indignantly.

He shrugged. 'I don't know. Maybe because you never quite know what I'll do or say next.' He grinned. 'Most girls seem to find that exciting.' He pulled her to her feet. 'Or could it be that you're afraid I might do this again?' He drew her close and kissed her soundly. 'You don't really dislike me all that much, do you Megan?' he asked looking down at her. 'Come on, why not admit it?'

She tried unsuccessfully to remove his arms from round her waist. 'Sometimes,' she said breathlessly. 'Sometimes you can be really impossible.'

He laughed softly. 'Oh come on – nothing and no one is ever impossible. I've lots of good qualities, you know. I think you should take time out to get to know me better.' He kissed her again and she felt herself beginning to melt as she had done on that day in the barn.

'What – what about Julia Simms?' she asked weakly.

He frowned. 'What does she have to do with it?'

'I thought she was your girl friend.'

'She is, but I have lots of girl friends,' he admitted. 'I don't see that they have anything to do with us – you and me.'

She pushed him firmly away. 'I think I'd

like another cup of coffee, please. And I think I've had enough of this conversation. I've never been one for casual relationships. As a matter of fact – I'm thinking of getting engaged.' She bit her lip the moment she had said it. What ever had got into her? Why had she said that?

He poured the coffee calmly. 'In that case, darling Megan – why are you here with me?'

She spun round to him. 'Because you asked me to come – to discuss a case!' she said hotly. 'How was I to know what you had in mind? I thought you would behave properly!'

'All right – all right, I apologise,' he said. 'I didn't intend to offend you. It was just that I got the distinct impression that day in the barn that you enjoyed being kissed by me.' He held up his hand as he saw her face colour. 'But we'll change the subject. Now, what was that you were telling me about your buying a new car?'

She took the cup of coffee from him and sat down. 'I'm going to buy Celia's,' she told him, glad to talk about something else. 'She's run into a little financial trouble over her grandmother's estate. She doesn't want to sell the cottage so she's going to give up her job for one nearer home and sell her car to me. Hopefully, that should do the trick.'

He nodded. 'I see. Where will she find work in Little Avedon though?'

'Oh, that's all fixed,' she told him. 'She's going to work for David Lattimer, the local G.P. He needs a receptionist. She has worked for him before as it happens, so it fits in nicely.'

'Ah yes, that would be when he was living at the surgery,' Jeff said. 'Before he bought Grey's Lodge from me.'

She stared at him. 'From – from *you?*'

'That's right,' he nodded. 'When I first came over to England I was mad to live in an English village in a really old house with roses round the door and all the trimmings. But life in Little Avedon drove me mad. I think it was the closeness of everything. I grew up with the nearest neighbours fifty miles away! So I sold Grey's to David Lattimer and moved in here. I find it–'

'Wait a minute, when was this?' she interrupted, her heart bumping wildly against her ribs.

'When?' he looked puzzled. 'Around last Easter, I guess – yes, it was March, I remember because– Hey where are you going?'

Megan had jumped up, her face very red, and was pulling on her coat. 'I have to go,' she said breathlessly. 'There's something I've just remembered. Thanks for the meal.'

'Wait! What's the matter?' He followed her to the door. 'When am I going to see you again, Megan?'

She rounded on him as she reached the door. 'I'd like to think *never!*' she said vehemently. 'I think you're totally unscrupulous and quite despicable – *Mr* Maitland. I was right about you from the start. Goodnight!' And so saying she ran out of the flat and down the stairs.

In the car she found that she was trembling and dangerously close to tears. Why hadn't she seen it before? It was so obvious. Jeff was the man who had let Caroline down so badly, not David at all! And here she was, about to make the most blundering mistake of her entire life!

CHAPTER FIVE

'So Mr Parkes, Gran's solicitor, says that with what I get for the car and the rest paid off in monthly instalments I should have paid off the debt in six months.' Celia looked expectantly at Megan who sat opposite her at the kitchen table, a mug of cocoa in her hands and a dreamy expression on her face. 'Megan,' she prompted. 'Are you all right? Did you hear what I said? I saw Mr Parkes today and he says it will be fine, the relatives have agreed to this method of paying off Gran's debt. I wanted you to know that it's largely thanks to you.'

Megan smiled. 'That's wonderful, though I haven't done anything really. Sorry if I seemed miles away.'

'Are you quite sure you're all right?' Celia asked again. Ever since she had come in this evening Megan had seemed odd; dazed and almost shocked looking.

Megan drank her cocoa down and leaned her elbows on the table. 'I've made rather a monumental decision this evening,' she confided. 'I've told David that I'll marry him.'

Celia's eyes opened wide. 'I'd no idea that things had progressed that far!'

'It *is* rather quick,' Megan agreed. 'But he seems sure enough.'

Celia shook her head. 'Wait a minute – I thought you'd gone out for a meal with Jeff Maitland tonight?'

Megan felt her cheeks colour. 'I did – but that was just to discuss a case. It was when I left him that I went round to David's. He asked me to marry him the other night, you see, and I said I'd think about it.'

'And you suddenly decided. What made your mind up so quickly?'

Megan sighed. 'It just struck me that I'd be a fool to let him go. I suppose any girl would jump at the chance to marry a man like David.'

'Mmm – I'm not sure that that's a good enough reason,' Celia said shaking her head. She looked closely at her friend. 'There's nothing wrong, is there? When you came in you looked, well, shaken to say the least!'

Megan laughed. 'Well, wouldn't you? I suppose I've been what's known as swept off my feet.'

Celia took the mugs to the sink and washed them thoughtfully. 'You asked me not very long ago how one knew when one was in love. I take it that now you know?'

'If you mean do I know what I'm doing the answer is yes.' Megan joined her at the sink and picked up a tea towel.

'Oh, I'm not trying to interfere,' Celia said quickly. 'It's just that I want you to be happy – both of you. When is the wedding to be?'

'Not for ages yet,' Megan assured her. 'There's so much to think about. What about you and Steve?' she asked in a desperate effort to change the subject.

'Steve will be home shortly,' Celia said with a sigh. 'This time there will be a lot to talk about. You know, although we've been engaged for almost two years we haven't seen each other more than a handful of times. It's no way for a romance to flourish.'

'Maybe you'll persuade him to get a shore job this time,' Megan said. But Celia didn't look very hopeful as she said:

'Yes, maybe I will.'

Megan had made the understatement of the year when she had said that there was a lot to think about. When she had left Jeff's flat in such a rush earlier that evening, she had gone to Grey's Lodge on impulse. In the same moment that she had realised that it had been Jeff and not David who had let

Caroline down she had also seen how easy it must have been for her to fall in love with him; how crushed she must have felt to discover that he had no more feeling for his women friends than he had for the car he drove or the cricket bat he handled with such efficiency. She realised how close she had come herself to falling into the same trap and it was with a feeling approaching blind panic that she had run straight to David Lattimer. David would never hurt her. He would cherish her and put her feelings above his own. If they married they would have a peaceful and fulfilling life together. He *wanted* to marry her – so why not?

When he had opened the door to her he had looked surprised, but had been even more amazed when she told him why she was there. Sweeping her into his arms he had kissed her and insisted that they go out to celebrate at once. They had had champagne and he had held her hand and told her that she was everything he had ever wanted. It should have been the most beautiful and memorable evening of her life. Could it have been the champagne or the suddenness of her decision that had made her feel so numb. She tried desperately to feel the excitement one read of in books at the prospect of becoming David's wife, but somehow her heart felt as dead as a stone. The only clear thought in her head was that she had done David a grave injustice in believing him to have treated Caroline badly. Now she must do all she could to make it up to him.

Lying in bed she tossed and turned, trying hard to sleep, but her mind was too active. She went over and over the events of the evening. Closing her eyes she tried to visualise David's face but all she saw were Jeff's mocking eyes – the way they had grown softer when he kissed her. She felt again the unrelenting hardness of his arms around her. With each unbidden thought she forced her mind back to David. Finally she fell into a restless sleep but dreamed of walking down the aisle in a white dress only to find that the man waiting for her at the altar was a total stranger. In a panic she fled from the church to find herself caught tightly in strong arms. She looked up and found herself looking straight into the laughing, mocking eyes of Jeff!

Waking with a start she found that she had overslept and so struggled out of bed to dress with a heavy heart and an aching head.

Thursday morning was the turn of the Health Centre clinic at Brinkdown, then afterwards she had a couple of house calls to make. One was on a middle-aged lady who was recovering from a stroke. She found her at the house of her married daughter, sitting alone at the window of the front room, staring out of the window at life outside like a bird in a cage. She waved and the woman's face lit up as she waved back. Her daughter opened the door.

'Mother's getting along nicely,' she told Megan briskly. 'But of course she'll never be the same again, will she?'

Megan stared at her. 'What makes you say that?'

'Well, it's brain damage, isn't it?' the woman said. 'It always leaves them a bit, well, slow.'

Megan fought back the annoyance that always hit her when she heard this kind of thing. 'Brain damage isn't always permanent,' she said patiently. 'Neither does it mean that the person is necessarily confused. There is a great deal we can do to help her back to recovery. May I see her, please?'

The woman opened the door to the room where her mother sat and Megan saw that the patient was a gentle, attractive woman in her mid fifties. She smiled. 'Good afternoon, Mrs Slater.'

'This is the speech therapist,' her daughter interrupted, speaking very loudly and with laborious distinction. 'She's going to help you to speak again – won't that be nice?' She turned to Megan. 'I'll leave you to it then,' she said. 'But you'll have a job getting through. Everything takes so long to sink in. I'm afraid I haven't always got the time.' And with these crushing words she went out, closing the door behind her. Megan fumed, especially when she saw the sad, lost look on the patient's face.

Half an hour later, after a rewarding and encouraging talk with Mrs Slater, Megan went in search of her daughter. She found her in the kitchen, baking, with the radio playing at full volume.

'May I have a word, Mrs Smith?' she asked, closing the door carefully.

Reluctantly the woman turned down the volume of the transistor. 'You won't mind if I get on, will you?' she said pointedly. 'I have a hungry family to feed.'

Megan looked at the row of greased tins. 'You know, your mother could quite easily help you with that,' she said. 'She should be occupied. She has the use of her hands and

I feel confident that she will be able to look after herself again providing she keeps in practice.' She glanced at the woman's face. 'She needs someone to talk to as well.'

Mrs Smith had the grace to look a little sheepish. 'I really am short of time,' she said. 'And like I said, everything takes so long to sink in. It's nerve racking when you're with it all day long.'

'It isn't really that it takes a long time to sink in,' Megan explained, 'it's just that she has trouble at the moment framing her replies to you. She'll need lots of practice. Your mother is suffering from what is known as aphasia. She knows perfectly well what you're saying to her and what she wants to say back, but it's all a little like a tangled ball of wool. It takes her time to unravel the tangle. It's very frustrating for her, especially when people just assume she hasn't understood and give up.'

The woman's face was red as she rolled her pastry fiercely. 'I don't take kindly to people coming here and lecturing me,' she said. 'It's hard enough with three kids and a husband, without having an invalid to take care of too. You should try it yourself sometime!'

Megan nodded understandingly. 'Of course it is. And I'm sorry if what I said sounded like a lecture. Anyone can see that you're doing a wonderful job in caring for your mother. All I wanted to point out to you is that she needn't *be* an invalid. With a little help and encouragement she could recover so well that she'll be able to go home and take up her normal life again. But speech and communication are important to her confidence and that's what I'm here to help you with.'

Mrs Smith brushed the flour from her hands and sat down opposite Megan. 'All right. What should I be doing that I'm not now?' she asked resignedly.

'Well, get her to involve herself more in what you're doing,' Megan suggested. 'You'll be surprised what a help she'll be. She isn't really confused, you know. Then, don't allow people to talk to her as though she's deaf and can't hear. That must be very hurtful. Give her all your attention when she's trying to speak to you and try not to let her feel that she's holding you up – even though she will be to start with. I think you'll consider it worth your while to let things slide a little for the sake of her recovery.'

Mrs Smith nodded. 'All right – I'll try.'

Something about the set of her shoulders and the tired lines round her mouth aroused Megan's sympathy and she said:

'Look, there's a day centre for the disabled at Brinkdown General. If I could get her a place there she could go for maybe a couple of mornings a week. They have occupational therapy and the company of other people. It would give you a break. What do you say?'

She was rewarded by a look of utter relief. 'Oh, could you really? That would be wonderful. It's not that I don't care about Mother – or feel sorry for her. It's just–'

Megan patted her shoulder as she stood up. 'I know. I'll see what I can do and I'll be in touch. In the meantime, why don't you make her a cup of tea and take it to her with one of those delicious little cakes? Better still ask her to join you out here and help you with the clearing up. No time like the present.'

Mrs Smith smiled. 'What about you staying for a cup?'

'Nothing I'd like better,' Megan said wistfully. 'But I can't stop now. Maybe next time.'

Back in the car she gave a sigh as her mind came back to her own problems. If only they could be solved as easily!

During the next two weeks she felt as though everything was getting away from her and being taken completely out of her hands.

David gave her a beautiful ruby ring that had belonged to his grandmother. Celia began to plan a party for them; the conversation centred round wedding dates and honeymoon locations. Sometimes she felt that she wanted to shout for someone to switch off her life while she sorted her feelings out. But most of the time she just tried not to think at all. It was easier that way.

Another letter came from Caroline. Now she began to mention Angus, a good-looking young vet whom she had met at the tennis club she had joined. He seemed to be all she had once thought her doctor was and for the first time in her life Megan began to be slightly irritated by her cousin. Here *she* was, having the most traumatic time, in all probability about to make a terrible hash of things all on account of Caroline, whilst the lady in question seemed to have forgotten all about her broken heart!

Celia worked out her notice at the hospital and began working for David. Megan found a buyer for her Mini and took over Celia's almost new Fiesta – so life went on. As much as she could, Megan avoided seeing Jeff, though it was inevitable that she occasionally ran into him on Wednesday afternoons when their clinics coincided at Kingscroft Cottage

Hospital. When she did she was polite but cool, while he simply seemed unconcerned.

The weekend of the engagement party came round. It was arranged for a Saturday evening and Megan had left the guest list to Celia. She was a little put out, therefore, to find that it included Jeff Maitland and 'friend'. When she pointed it out to Celia she laughed.

'I put "friend" because you never know who the current one is,' she laughed. 'Julia Simms seems to have lasted longer than most, but you never know with Jeff.'

'Is he really such a Casanova?' Megan asked tartly.

Celia pulled a face. 'If you ask me, I think he considers that there's safety in numbers. He's just a tiny bit afraid.'

Megan shook her head. 'I can't agree. That sounds most unlike him. I wouldn't have thought that anything frightened Jeff Maitland – especially women!'

'Mmm – I wouldn't like to bet on it,' Celia said. 'He was almost hooked by a young teacher when he was living here in the village. She really had him by the nose. You ought to have seen him!'

Megan stared at her. 'Are we talking about Jeff?'

Celia nodded. 'Really. Mind you, she was a very strong personality, a really bossy type. If he'd married her it would have been Samson and Delilah all over again. I think he had a lucky escape!'

She busied herself with the canapés she was making for the party while Megan stared out of the window, bread knife in hand. There was little doubt that Celia had been talking about Caroline. But surely it was incredible – Caroline, bossy, a strong personality! In her bag was the letter she had received two days ago, in reply to the one she wrote to tell her of her engagement. Now she recalled bits of it:

'Congratulations! I knew David Lattimer slightly when I was there. He is a very nice person. It has always puzzled me that you wanted to go to Little Avedon. Personally, I found it a dead and alive sort of place. Up here it is so much better. I wish you could come up this summer, Meg, and meet all the new friends I have made, especially Angus. I really believe that this time I am in love, Meg–' Megan sighed. It all sounded so familiar; it could almost have been the same letter Caroline had written when she first came to Little Avedon, except that then she was extolling the virtues of the village instead of running it down!

The first party guest to arrive was Jane Lang. She had had her throat condition confirmed and was waiting for a bed at Brinkdown General for her operation. But she seemed quite cheerful as she chatted to the girls in the kitchen, helping them to carry the last of the plates of food through into the living room.

'Will Jeff Maitland be doing your op', Jane?' Celia asked.

Jane shook her head. 'A Mr Oldershaw from Gloucester is doing it. That's why I have to wait for a while. But Jeff says he's a first class man, the best in his field, very experienced in this op'.'

Megan said nothing. She knew that it was a tricky and delicate operation and she didn't blame Jeff for wanting to pass it on to an older and more experienced man, but it sounded so unlike brash, confident Jeff Maitland. She would have thought he'd have welcomed the opportunity to show off his skill.

David arrived, bringing her a bouquet of flowers and other guests followed soon after, all of them congratulating the newly engaged couple, admiring Megan's ring and chatting about wedding plans. Once more Megan had the cold feeling deep inside her that things were getting out of hand. Before she knew it she'd be married, she told herself. But that was what she wanted, wasn't it?

Jeff arrived with Julia Simms. As usual they were late and Jeff caught Megan unawares as she was making fresh punch in the kitchen.

'So here you are – the blushing bride-to-be,' he said mockingly, picking up a glass. 'When you told me that you were thinking of getting engaged I didn't take you seriously – and I certainly never imagined that it was David. I thought it'd be the boy-next-door from back home. Wasn't it all rather quick?'

To divert attention from the blush that crept up her neck she ladled punch into the glass he held and he raised an eyebrow at her.

'What's this for – to drink your health in?' He raised the glass. 'Here's to you – and rather you than me!'

'What does that mean?' she asked.

He laughed. 'The marriage bit. Tie myself to one woman for the rest of my life? I can't think of a worse fate! It'd be like being cast adrift on a raft with a gorilla!'

'I can see that any girl contemplating marriage with you might view it like that,' she returned hotly. 'But I'm sure you have no need to worry. You have a manner guaranteed to put any sane girl off!'

He put his head on one side and moved closer to her. 'What's that quotation? "Methinks the lady does protest too much". It's funny how wrong one can be. You know I would have sworn that at one point I had you interested in me.'

Warm colour flooded her cheeks. 'What an idea! How do you manage to be so conceited?'

He ginned unrepentantly. 'I've had a long time to work on it!'

David put his head round the door. 'Want any help with that punch?' He looked at Jeff. 'I hope you're not chatting up my fiancée behind my back.'

Jeff laughed. 'As if I would! Actually I was just waiting for you to put in an appearance. I wanted to ask your permission to kiss the bride-to-be. Do I have it?'

David smiled good-naturedly. 'Of course. I can afford to be generous now, can't I? I'm only surprised that you *asked!*'

Jeff seized Megan round the waist and drew her to him. His lips came down hard on hers till she felt as though she were drowning. Angrily she pushed him away, glaring from one man to the other.

'You could have asked *my* permission!' she said furiously. 'Nobody owns me yet. I object to being passed around like a – like a parcel!' and with that she rushed out of the room and up the stairs.

In her room she sat on the bed, her heart pounding and hot tears blurring her vision. Why couldn't he have stayed away? But, of course, he wasn't to know the effect he had on her. To him it was all a game and she was just another girl like all the others. But deep inside a disturbing thought nagged at her: Why couldn't David's kiss thrill her the way Jeff's did? David's kiss meant love and tenderness, not just the satisfying of a sensual whim. To David it mattered that it was her – to Jeff, anyone would do. He had made that abundantly clear, he had actually said so – well, as good as. She took a deep breath and swallowed hard. She would – she *must* put him out of her mind!

A tap on the door startled her and she hastily dabbed at her eyes as a fiery head came round the door.

'Oh – I'm sorry, dear. I didn't know any-one was in here. I was looking for a place to powder my nose.' It was Sister McNab.

Megan forced a smile.

'Of course, come in. I – I came up to change my tights – a ladder,' she said, feeling the need for explanation.

But Sister McNab seemed to notice nothing amiss as she sat at the dressing table and took out her powder compact.

'Actually, I'm glad of this opportunity to have a word with you, dear,' she said. 'I'm a little worried about Jane. It's this operation she's to have. She's more bothered about it than she's letting on.'

Megan nodded. 'It must be worrying for her. But she seems cheerful enough.'

The sister put away her make-up and turned to look at Megan. 'I know you'll understand because you've been in the same position. She has no parents, you see. In fact no family at all. She was an only child and her parents were both killed in an accident just after she qualified. She's alone in the world and in dire need of an understanding friend of her own age to talk to.'

'Of course,' Megan said, immediately concerned for the girl. 'But I would have thought that an outgoing girl like Jane would have heaps of friends.'

The sister sighed. 'She has – of a kind. But you know what people are; they're used to

128

Jane being bright and cheery, making them laugh. A Jane who's quiet and apprehensive makes them uneasy – someone to steer clear of.'

Megan frowned. 'How callous!'

'Ah well, I suppose one can't pass judgments,' Sister McNab said tolerantly. 'To some folk illness is terrifying.' She smiled. 'Anyway, see what you can do to take her mind off things if you get the chance, eh?'

The sister's words took Megan's thoughts away from her own problems for a while. Downstairs, she mingled again with the guests, seeking out Jane when she caught sight of her across the room. They talked about some of the cases they had both treated at Kingscroft, then Megan suggested that Jane might be interested in a lecture that was being given at Brinkdown Health Centre the following week.

'We might go together,' she said. 'Then maybe have a coffee afterwards.'

Jane seemed delighted. 'You could come back to my flat. I'd like you to see it,' she said. 'I've decorated it myself and I'm quite proud of it.'

David came up and slipped an arm round Megan's waist.

'I've been looking everywhere for you,' he

smiled down at her. 'Come and be introduced to Mrs Thorne, the headmistress of the village school. She says she hasn't met you yet.'

Mrs Thorne was a tall, rather elegant lady with soft grey hair and twinkling blue eyes. Megan had seen her often in the village and knew her to pass the time of day with but as yet they had not been introduced. She smiled as she shook hands with Megan.

'I've been meaning to come across and make myself known,' she said apologetically. 'But school life is so hectic at this time of year. Thank goodness it will soon be the holidays.'

'I know how you feel,' Megan said. 'I have a cousin who is a teacher and she gets very jaded towards the end of term.'

'Do you like this part of the world?' Mrs Thorne asked.

'Very much. Though of course my work is the same where ever I go,' Megan told her.

'I know what you mean,' Mrs Thorne nodded. 'It doesn't always apply though, you know. On the whole I prefer local teachers in the school; those who understand local children and their ways. It makes a great difference with the little ones especially. You can't treat country children the same as town ones, their whole background and environment is totally different, even in this day and age.' She smiled reminiscently. 'I had a young teacher recently who just couldn't understand this. She looked such an angelic girl and yet she made more disruptions in the school than I'd had in ten years or more!'

Megan felt her colour rising. Was this Caroline again? 'Oh – in what way?' she asked.

Mrs Thorne shook her head. 'It sounds funny, but she overdid the discipline. Make no mistake, I'm all for it, but you can have too much of a good thing. No doubt she'd done her teaching practice in city schools where it was sorely needed, but here it isn't – well, not to that extent.' She laughed. 'Sometimes I think that those small delicate-looking people feel the need to assert themselves more than most and often end up aggressive.' She raised her eyes to the ceiling. 'I had more parents round to complain than I ever remember. A pity, because apart from that one fault she was a very good teacher.'

Megan moved away as the conversation came to an end. She was puzzled. That was the second time this evening that she had heard Caroline described in this way. It was true that she had seen little of her while she was at college, or since either. Could she possibly have been prejudiced, have been seeing her cousin through rose-coloured spectacles? Blinded by the remembered image of that lost little motherless child of long ago? Whatever the answer she had certainly been given something to think about this evening.

David found her again, taking the empty glass from her hand and leading her firmly towards the open French windows.

'I've hardly seen anything of you this evening,' he whispered in her ear. 'And now I'm determined to have you to myself for five minutes.'

They walked out into the warm velvet darkness and David drew a deep breath of the evening air. 'Ah – that's better.' He lifted her chin with the tip of his finger and looked into her eyes. 'Are you happy, darling?'

She nodded. 'Of course, why do you ask?'

He shrugged. 'Just a feeling. You've seemed a little preoccupied, looked a bit wistful. And earlier I thought you were upset when you rushed upstairs. Is there anything you'd like to talk about?'

She put her arms around his waist and leaned her head against his chest. He was so understanding. She must be quite mad to have any doubts.

'No,' she said. 'It's nothing – just that I'm not much of a party girl. I'm not at my best in crowds.'

His arms folded round her and he kissed her forehead. 'Well, that's fine with me. Who needs crowds?' he said softly.

Together they strolled down to the end of the garden, to where a huge sycamore tree cast its dappled shadow over everything. There he took her in his arms and kissed her deeply.

'Don't let's leave it too long now before the wedding,' he said. 'Neither of us has any family to bother about. We could arrange it for as soon as we like – say a month from today, for instance?' He looked down at her and she was grateful for the shadows hiding the look of sheer panic she knew she must be wearing.

'A month!' she protested. 'But there's so much to think about.'

'Not really. We already have somewhere to live – unless of course you'd rather look for another house, a more modern one. As for the wedding itself, there won't be very many people to invite, so it should be fairly straightforward.'

Megan bit her lip. 'Of course I don't want a modern house but – I do have some relatives actually, well, a cousin. She's in Scotland at the moment and I don't know whether she'll be able to get away, and I couldn't possibly be married without her being there. We're very close.'

He laughed softly. 'All right, darling. But you'd better write to her at once and find out. Have you thought where you'd like to go for the honeymoon? What about the Greek Islands?'

Megan took his arm. 'I think we should be getting inside again. I'm sure I just felt a spot of rain. Besides, the others will be wondering where we are. We can talk about the honeymoon another time.'

Reluctantly he allowed her to steer him towards the lighted windows again and she heaved a sigh of relief. If only he wouldn't try to hurry her so. There had been no time at all for her to grow accustomed to the idea of marriage – and she needed time, a lot of it. As they reached the little gate that led onto the lawn David stopped and drew her once more into his arms, finding her lips once more. But as they drew apart she heard a movement over by the apple tree and caught sight of two figures out of the corner of her eye. Turning

134

her head she saw Jeff Maitland and Julia Simms clasped in a close embrace. David laughed softly.

'Let's go. I'm afraid we're in the way. You know, it wouldn't surprise me if there wasn't another engagement announced soon.'

'If you mean Jeff Maitland I can assure you that it's very unlikely,' she said sharply. 'Jeff has far too low an opinion of women in general to tie himself down to one of them for life. He told me earlier this evening that marriage was like being cast adrift on a raft with a gorilla!'

David exploded with laughter, his shoulders shaking and Megan felt herself growing hot with annoyance. 'Personally, I don't see the joke!' she said stiffly.

He put his arm round her. 'You would if you knew Jeff as well as I do,' he said mildly. He felt her trembling and looked down at her with concern. 'Darling, are you cold?'

'A little,' she said. But she wouldn't have admitted for the world, either to him or to herself, the real reason for the tremor that ran through her body. Never in a million years would she own up to the jealous ache that ate at her heart when she saw Julia Simms in the arms she herself longed to be in.

CHAPTER SIX

The lecture at Brinkdown Health Centre was on the treatment of spastics and of interest to both Megan and Jane Lang. Megan was using her new car now and called for Jane at her flat in Kingscroft. On the way the girls chatted, though Jane's voice was still very hoarse and she was trying to rest it as much as she could out of working hours. She confided to Megan that she was not looking forward to being out of action.

'I was so relieved that the trouble was nothing more serious,' she said. 'Being on your own is no joke when it comes to being ill.'

'I think I can speak for all of us when I promise that you won't be neglected,' Megan told her.

Jane smiled. 'That's very sweet of you. And of course I know that I have some very good friends. No, what worried me was that I might not be able to get back to work – might not be able to support myself.'

Megan took her eyes off the road for a

moment to stare at Jane in dismay. 'Oh dear – we *have* been having some morbid thoughts, haven't we?'

Jane looked slightly embarrassed. 'I know it's silly now, but all sorts of things go through your head when you have no one to talk to and you can't sleep at night.'

'I'm lucky. I have a cousin who is more like a sister,' Megan told her. 'We were brought up together, so when my parents died we had each other.'

Jane looked thoughtful. 'That's funny. There was a girl Jeff Maitland was going around with a while ago – she was in the same situation. He brought her to the hospital dance last year and we got into conversation. She was a very pretty girl, blonde and fragile looking, though Jeff said she had a will of iron and liked things all her own way. She told me that she had a cousin she'd been brought up with but that she'd been glad to get away from her. All the "mothering" she got from her stifled her. It just shows, doesn't it, how very different people can be. Oh!–' She gasped as Megan took a corner too fast.

'I'm sorry – that's what comes of not concentrating.' Megan apologised. 'I'm not quite used to this new car yet.'

They drove on in silence, Jane afraid she

was talking too much and taking Megan's attention away from her driving; Megan boiling at what she had just heard. There could be no doubt that, once more, the person they were talking about was Caroline. It was as though she were getting to know her cousin for the first time! The girl she had known from childhood, had always shielded and protected at the expense of living a life of her own, seemed all at once a stranger to her! Maybe it *was* a claustrophobic feeling, being looked after so intensively. But what a way to find out!

'I understand that Jeff almost married her – this girl you were telling me about,' she said at length.

Jane looked up, a wry smile on her face. 'I think she had her eye on him,' she said. 'And as I said, she liked to get her own way, that must have been one of the bad habits her cousin got her into! But Jeff never had marriage on his mind. I don't think he ever will. He's a good doctor. It's said that he's one of the best E.N.T. men we've had at Kingscroft. And he's a great person, but when it comes to women–'

'He treats them like dirt!' Megan finished for her.

Jane frowned. 'Oh no. I wouldn't say that.

As long as you know where you are – and you always do with Jeff – you can be sure of a great time and a lot of fun. He just doesn't have any intention of being tied down, that's all.'

'You sound as though you speak from experience,' Megan said.

Jane nodded. 'Yes, I've been out with Jeff once or twice.' She glanced at Megan. 'I believe you have too. Did he do something to upset you?'

Megan felt her cheeks burning. 'No, of course not. I only really met him in the course of work anyway – and at Celia's parties. It was just that I got the impression that – oh well, it doesn't matter.'

Jane smiled. 'When can we expect to hear wedding bells for you and David?'

'Not until next year if I get my way,' Megan told her. 'David is all for rushing things but I want to take my time, collect a trousseau and so on.'

'If I'd managed to land a gorgeous man like David I think I'd be inclined to snap him up quickly!' Jane joked. 'Don't you realise that you're the envy of all the marriageable ladies in the county?'

Megan laughed. 'All the same, I'll take my time.'

The lecture was interesting and gave the girls plenty to discuss on the way home. They had coffee afterwards at Jane's flat which was quite close to the hospital and Megan admired the two neat rooms, kitchen and bathroom.

'I'd have liked one like this myself,' she said. 'If I hadn't been lucky enough to find Celia and her cottage.'

'And you'll soon be moving into that beautiful old house of David's,' Jane reminded her. 'You really are a lucky girl, Megan.'

'Yes,' Megan agreed. 'I suppose I am.' She wished she could feel as convinced as she sounded.

After she had left Jane that night Megan had a lot to think about. All at once it seemed that she didn't know Caroline at all! It was certainly true that all their lives she had protected her, from their first day at school up to the time when Caroline had gone away to college. It had seemed the natural way of things – to both of them. Had college given Caroline a new view of life? She wished she were here so that they could talk about it. Maybe if she wrote to her they could arrange a meeting. It hurt to know that she had been talked about by her cousin, even though not by name. And it angered her that Caroline had not had the courage to face her with her grievance instead of going behind her back.

Later, as she lay in bed she thought over the past years; of the way she had always stood down in favour of Caroline, given her first choice, made sure she always had everything she wanted. Could it have been claustrophobic? Could she have been pressing her into a mould that was against her nature? And this move – coming to Little Avedon expressly to punish a man who had hurt her. In the darkness she suddenly blushed with shame. How stupid it seemed now, especially in view of the catastrophic mistake she had made in confusing the two men!

As soon as it was light she got up and made herself a pot of tea. She would ring Caroline as soon as it was decently possible and ask her to meet her. Possibly they could each travel as far as London and have a day together there. If they were to remain good friends this rift between them must be healed.

Megan sipped her tea and the clock crept round. At last it was seven o'clock and she went into the hall and dialled the number. It was answered almost at once by Hester:

'Hello – Fort William 5906. Hester Mc-Donald speaking.'

'Hester – it's Megan. Is Caroline there?'

'Oh dear, nothing wrong, I hope?'

'No. It's just that I wanted to talk to her and it's the only time I can be sure of finding her in,' Megan said with sudden inspiration. She heard Hester's sigh of relief.

'Well, thank goodness for that! Phone calls at this time of the morning are a bit like telegrams, they always make me think the worst,' she said. 'Hang on, dear. I'll just give her a call.'

When she came to the phone, Caroline sounded carefree and happy: 'Hello, Meg. What is it that's got you out of bed so early?'

'You, mainly,' Megan said tartly. 'Look, Caro, can you come down to London this weekend? I want to see you.'

Caroline laughed. 'What's the matter? You sound as though the world has fallen apart – and you a newly engaged woman!'

'Please, Caro – there's something I have to discuss with you and it won't wait.' There was a pause at the other end, then Caroline said:

'Well, you probably won't believe this, but Angus and I were coming down anyway, to spend the weekend. Can you come up for the day on Saturday?'

Megan hesitated. 'I rather wanted to see you on your own.'

'That's all right. Angus has some business to attend to on Saturday. We could talk while he was doing that. It's too good an opportunity to miss, Meg. Do come.'

It was not at all what she wanted, but she could see that it would have to do, so she agreed: 'All right then. I'll find out the time of my train and let you know. Perhaps you could meet me at the station.'

As she replaced the receiver she turned to find Celia standing at the foot of the stairs. She sighed and pushed her tousled hair out of her eyes. 'I've just been making arrangements to meet my cousin in London on Saturday,' she explained.

Celia looked at her. 'Is anything wrong? You look as though you haven't slept much.'

Megan shrugged. 'It's nothing that isn't my own fault.' It was impossible to explain fully to Celia so she laughed lightly. 'Call it the maternal instinct if you like. I just want to reassure myself that she's all right.'

In the kitchen Celia took in the cold teapot and the used cup on the table. She turned to Megan.

'Look – tell me to mind my own business if you feel like it, but if there's anything wrong I'd like to feel that you could talk to me.'

Quite suddenly Megan felt overwhelmed and she sat down at the table, a lump filling her throat. 'I know – and it's kind of you, Celia. But I can't explain to you. Too many people are involved. It seems I've spent most of my life barking up the wrong tree, that's all and it all seems such a waste.'

Celia sat down opposite her. 'It's nothing to do with David, is it?'

Looking up and meeting Celia's candid eyes, Megan sighed. 'In a way, yes. Though he's one of the best things to come out of it all. I'm determined to make him as happy as I can.'

'I see.' Celia got up and began to prepare the breakfast. 'Well, that's all right then. I won't pry, Megan, but if you do want someone to talk to – any time – you know I'm here.'

It was Wednesday and when Megan arrived at Kingscroft Cottage Hospital that afternoon she found Jeff Maitland waiting for her in her room. At the unexpected sight of him she caught her breath.

'Oh! – Jeff. Good afternoon.'

He bowed to her with the old hint of mockery. 'Good afternoon, Miss Lacey. I was just writing a note to leave on your desk. It was about a meeting next week to introduce the new combined clinic. Yes–' he grinned. 'It's coming off. The meeting is in the lecture hall at the health centre – Monday evening at seven-thirty. I hope you can make it.'

She nodded. 'I'll be there.'

'Good.' He watched her as she took off her coat and sorted through the notes on her desk. His eyes unnerved her and she tried to ignore him without success. At last she glanced up to see that he was looking at her with some concern, his usually humorous eyes serious for once.

'Megan – you don't look yourself. Are you well?'

'Perfectly, thank you.' She continued with her preparation for the afternoon's work, but he perched on a corner of her desk.

'Look – tell me to go to hell if you like, but I have to say this: I think you're making a mistake.'

She looked up at him, her eyes wide with astonishment. 'May I ask in what way?'

His brows came together angrily. 'You can drop the Miss Icicle bit. You know damned well what I'm talking about. You're worried sick about something and I'm pretty sure I know what it is.' He stood up. 'I'll pick you up after clinic and we'll go back to my place. We can talk there.'

She thought she would burst with fury. 'Let's get one thing clear, once and for all,' she said, her voice trembling. 'I do *not* want to talk to you about anything – now or at any time. And why you should concern yourself with my private affairs is quite beyond me!'

But her tone did nothing to deter him. 'Someone has to sort you out,' he said calmly. 'Especially as you're obviously incapable of looking after yourself. See you later.' He would have swept out of the room in his customary manner but she stood up, panic filling her throat and chest as she almost screamed at him:

'*Wait!* Don't expect me to be here – don't expect me to go anywhere with you – now or at any other time because I *won't*. I – I mean it. Do you understand?'

He stopped in his tracks and turned to stare at her uncomprehendingly. 'Oh Megan – Megan, love, something is very wrong, isn't it? Very wrong indeed.'

The softening of his voice and the look in

his eyes were almost more than she could bear and she gripped the edge of the desk till her knuckles showed white, in an effort to stop the tears from falling. 'Please, Jeff, leave me alone – *please.*' The last word was no more than a whisper and he came slowly towards her across the room.

'Don't,' he said, touching her shoulder. 'Don't take on like that. I didn't mean to upset you. I just thought you might need a friend to talk to. I thought you and I were mates.' His mouth curved in a hint of the old audacious grin. 'Though right now I seem more like the enemy! Just what have I done, Megan? Would you mind telling me? There's always been something, hasn't there? Yet as far as I'm aware I've done nothing to annoy you.'

'It's – I–' Her mouth opened and shut helplessly as she cast about for words, but just at that moment she was saved by the timely appearance of Sister McNab who tapped briefly on the door and bustled in bearing a sheaf of papers.

'I expect you were looking for these,' she said, casting a disapproving look at Jeff. 'I believe they're looking everywhere for you, Mr Maitland,' she said looking at her watch. 'It's well past time for starting.'

With a last resigned look at Megan he left the room.

When her clinic was over she left the hospital like a fugitive, creeping along the corridor, expecting to find Jeff lurking behind every corner. Once in the car she lost no time in leaving the car park and the town behind her. How could she ever hope to begin explaining to Jeff, even if she wanted to? Besides, the fact remained, he was fickle and brash. He thought women were there for the convenience and amusement of men. How could he be expected to understand either Caroline's broken heart, or her attempts at avenging it? It would no doubt be a subject of great hilarity to him.

When the train drew into Paddington station at ten-thirty, Megan felt her heart quicken. It was not going to be easy, this meeting with Caroline. How had she failed to see that her whole attitude had been wrong all these years? That instead of being a caring, loving person she had been nothing but a drag and a bore, inhibiting her cousin and spoiling her enjoyment of life.

She saw her almost as soon as she stepped down from the train, looking fitter and prettier than ever, wearing a deep lilac-coloured suit and with her soft blonde hair framing her face like a pale gold halo. In spite of her feelings, Megan felt the familiar rush of affection as she held out her hands.

'Caro – it's good to see you. How well you look!'

Caroline kissed her, then, looking more closely at her she frowned. 'Well, I'm sorry, Meg, but I'm afraid it's more than can be said for you. You look positively washed out! What has David Lattimer been doing to you?'

Megan shook her head. 'I expect I'm just a bit tired. Can we go and have a coffee somewhere? I'm dying for one.'

'Yes, of course.' Caroline took her arm. 'Angus is meeting us for lunch later. I thought we'd have ample time for our pow-wow.'

They found a café and ordered coffee. Megan was dismayed to find that she was to have so little time to talk to Caroline, but it seemed there was nothing for it but to try to fit in all she had to say. Taking a deep draught of her coffee she began:

'You're happy then, up there in Scotland? Away from me, I mean, because that was the idea really, wasn't it?'

The smile vanished from Caroline's face.

'What do you mean? Who's been talking to you?'

'What I've heard was purely by accident,' Megan told her. 'You see, no one knows that we're related in Little Avedon.' She smiled and touched her cousin's hand. 'Why didn't you tell me I was stifling you, Caro? It would have saved a lot of heartache.'

Caroline took a deep breath, then looked at Megan. 'I don't know when it began,' she said. 'When the "mothering" became "smothering". I only know that when it did I couldn't get away fast enough. That's why I was glad to go to college.' She looked at Megan hesitantly. 'I hope you don't mind me saying this, Meg?'

Megan shook her head. 'It has to be said. I only wish it hadn't all got so out of hand.'

'All that protection,' Caroline went on: 'It didn't help my character at all, you know. Once I got away from you and found that people weren't falling over themselves to please me I became aggressive and bossy. I thought the world was mine and that other people were in it simply to dance attendance on me.' She smiled wryly. 'I must have been a real pain in the neck! – till Angus came along that was. He soon showed me the error of my ways. I hated him for it at first, but now

– well, that's why we're here – to buy a ring and celebrate our engagement.' She held out her hand to display a twinkling diamond. 'So that makes two of us. Isn't it wonderful?'

Megan took one look at her cousin's ring, then at her radiant face, and, to her own horror and Caroline's, she burst into tears. As she rummaged in her handbag for a hanky she apologised: 'I'm sorry. Take no notice – I don't know what's the matter with me–'

Caroline touched her hand. 'What is it, Meg? It's not like you to be weepy. Something else has upset you, hasn't it?'

Megan looked up at her cousin. 'You really have grown up, haven't you? You really don't need me any more? You haven't for a long time. What a fool I was not to see it!'

'It's high time you had a life of your own,' Caroline said softly. 'Now tell me, when are you planning to get married?'

Megan closed her eyes in an attempt to stop fresh tears from falling. 'That's just it,' she said. 'I didn't plan to get married at all. I've committed myself to it because of something I was trying to do for you!'

Caroline was clearly mystified. 'For *me?* But how could you? I'm afraid I don't understand.'

'Of course you don't. I'm not at all sure that I do myself now that I come to look back on it all. I must have been mad!' Megan admitted. 'If you ask me, *I* was the one who needed to grow up!' She blew her nose and put away her handkerchief. 'When I knew that you had been made so unhappy in the Cotswolds, by some brute of a man, I made up my mind to go there, find him, and teach him the lesson of his life.'

'Oh, Meg, you didn't!' Caroline stared at her. 'But you didn't even know who the man was, so how could you?'

'I thought I knew enough to find him,' Megan told her. 'I knew that he lived in the oldest house in the village and that he was a doctor. I thought that was enough.'

Realisation spread over Caroline's face and her hand flew to her mouth. 'Oh! You must have thought it was David Lattimer!' She laughed. 'Still, it all turned out happily in the end, didn't it?'

'Not altogether,' Megan said. 'I intended to let him down as he had let you down. Then I found out that he was the wrong man! Now I feel responsible. I feel I must go through with it and try to make him happy.'

Caroline shook her head gravely. 'I think you're playing with fire, Meg. You'll both get hurt if it isn't right. Oh Meg, what a mess!' She poured two more cups of coffee and they sat sipping them in silence.

'Were you very much in love with Jeff Maitland?' Megan asked at length.

Caroline looked up. 'Oh, you found out it was him then?' She shrugged. 'I *thought* I was at the time, but now I've met Angus I know what the real thing is like.' She laughed. 'I think Jeff's main attraction was that he made himself so hard to get. I don't think any woman will ever get him. That, for me, made him well nigh irresistible!'

Megan looked at her cousin. She seemed so happy and confident; so sure of what she wanted from life and where she was going. 'Caro,' she whispered. 'What shall I do?'

Caroline smiled tenderly. 'That's the first time you've ever asked my advice. Poor Meg. You're going to have to break it off with David and tell him the truth. I know it won't be easy, but I think it's the only way.'

Megan nodded. 'I think you're right. But I wish the next few weeks were over.'

When they met Angus for lunch Megan found him to be a large young man with sandy hair and candid grey eyes. He obviously adored Caroline and yet seemed very good at keeping her in line, which in her turn she clearly enjoyed. He had booked seats for the matinée performance of a well acclaimed play and the three of them enjoyed themselves very much indeed. Afterwards there was just time for a light meal before it was time for Megan to catch the train back. As it began to move out of the station, Caroline caught at her hand.

'You will write and let me know how things go, won't you?' she said. 'I feel partly responsible. I'm glad we've had this talk, Meg. I feel I can really look on you as an adoptive sister now, instead of some sort of surrogate "mum".' She began to run to keep pace with the moving train. 'God bless,' she said. 'Take care of yourself.'

Leaning out of the window, Megan watched till the two waving figures on the platform were out of sight, then she sat down in her corner seat and tried hard to read the magazine Angus had bought her, swallowing hard at the stubborn lump in her throat. The task ahead of her was too daunting to contemplate at the moment.

When the train drew into Kingscroft station David was there to meet her. As she stepped down from the train he kissed her lightly.

'Had a nice day, darling?'

She nodded. 'Very. My cousin broke the

news of her engagement, so it was something of a celebration.'

He pulled her hand through his arm. 'How about doing a little celebrating of our own?'

Megan's heart sank. If they were to spend the evening together she would feel obliged to tell him that their engagement was a mistake and the reason why – and she didn't feel at all equal to it at the moment.

'Would you mind if I went straight home, David?' she asked haltingly. 'I have rather a headache.'

'Of course,' he said understandingly. 'You've had a long day. I'll take you home right away.'

When they reached the cottage she felt obliged to ask him in for coffee but he refused. 'Not tonight. You have an early night. You've been looking peaky lately.' He leaned across and took her gently in his arms. 'You are happy about our engagement, aren't you, Megan?'

She hesitated. 'Are you, David?'

His eyes searched hers. 'Have you any particular reason for asking that?'

She bit her lip. 'As a matter of fact – yes.' Maybe this was the right time. Maybe here, in the dim closeness of the car she could tell him the whole truth with as little pain as possible – praying to Heaven that he would understand and forgive her. Though God knew she didn't deserve to be forgiven. She took a deep breath.

'David – there's something I must tell you–'

Her words were drowned by an urgent tapping on the car window and she turned to see Celia standing by the car in the gathering dusk.

'I'm sorry, but there's an urgent message for David,' she said. 'Doctor Banks from Coltsworth is out on a call and it looks as though the Johnson baby is on its way. I've been trying everywhere to reach you, David. I even rang the station.'

Megan got hurriedly out of the car as David started the engine. 'I'll ring you!' he called. 'Thanks, Celia!' And with a roar and a cloud of dust he was on his way. Celia glanced apologetically at Megan.

'I'm sorry about that, but the Johnsons live right out in the wilds, about six miles from anywhere. The call came in about an hour ago. It's Mrs Johnson's fourth and she's had all the others quickly, so I knew it was urgent.'

'Don't apologise. I only hope he's in time,' Megan said. Together they went indoors and Celia smiled as she helped Megan take off her coat.

'Well, after all that panic, what sort of day did you have?'

'Oh, very nice, thank you,' Megan said non-committally. 'And you?'

Celia sighed. 'I had a call from Steve as a matter of fact.'

'Steve? I thought he wasn't due home for a couple of weeks yet.'

'That's what I thought too. But it seems there was some mix up over cargoes so they missed out two ports of call. He's changing ships too, so he has an extra week's leave.'

'Where is he now, then?' Megan asked.

'At home with his parents in Brinkdown for the weekend,' Celia told her. 'Then he's coming here.'

Megan frowned. Celia didn't look as pleased as she should under the circumstances. 'Aren't you excited?' she asked. 'Nothing's gone wrong, has it?'

Celia sat down suddenly at the table, twisting the ring on her finger and biting her lip hard to stop it from trembling. 'Oh Megan,' she said brokenly. 'I don't know what to do. You see I – I don't love Steve any more! How can I tell him? What am I to say?'

CHAPTER SEVEN

Megan looked at her friend helplessly. 'You – you don't love him? When did you discover that?'

Celia looked up at her, twisting her handkerchief. 'I suppose if I'm honest I've known deep inside for some time. It was just when I heard his voice this morning that I realised I couldn't let it go on.' She sighed. 'I told you that being parted for months on end was no way for a romance to flourish.'

Megan sat down. 'You'll have to tell him as soon as possible, of course. Oh, but maybe when you see him again you'll feel different,' she added hopefully.

But Celia shook her head. 'No – no, I won't, I'm really sure about it. I've never been surer of anything in my life.' She groaned. 'I'm certainly not looking forward to telling Steve though.'

Megan frowned. 'What has happened to make you realise so suddenly? I mean, apart from complaining about the partings, you've said nothing before.'

Celia avoided her eyes. 'I've just pushed the doubts to the back of my mind – refused to face them, I suppose. Then you and David got engaged and I saw the way things were with you. I knew then that Steve and I weren't right for each other. He'll never give up the sea, I realise that. It wouldn't be fair to ask him when it's the life he loves. But I know now that I couldn't stand that kind of marriage.'

'Perhaps you're wrong though,' Megan pressed. 'Suppose – just suppose he did get a shore job. How would you feel then?'

Celia lifted her shoulders. 'It's no good. It's over.'

'When romance – *love* – dies there's nothing that will resurrect it, is there?'

'I suppose not.' Megan sighed. 'Look, why don't you sleep on it? Wait till you see him.' But although Celia nodded and agreed that she would do this it was obvious that her mind was irrevocably made up.

Later, when she was alone, Megan thought of how similar their positions were. She too was going to have to break off her engagement and hurt a person of whom she had become fond; she too dreaded the thought of doing it. If only she could tell Celia so and share the burden. It was ironic to think that it was her own engagement that had made up Celia's mind for her! Megan couldn't help feeling that here were two more people she had indirectly made unhappy. What a fool she had been to meddle in something which, she knew now, had never really concerned her.

Celia and David were both working all day on Sunday; David was on call and Celia was putting in a voluntary day to catch up with the paperwork that had been neglected over the months that David had been without a receptionist. Megan worked away at home, preparing equipment for some new experiments she meant to try out at the following week's clinics. She also cooked the meals which the three of them ate together.

It was on Monday morning when she was packing her case for the day that Celia looked up in surprise.

'What on earth are those?' she asked.

Megan laughed and slipped her hand into one of the glove puppets she had made. 'Good morning, Miss Morris,' she said in a squeaky voice. 'I'm Henry Horse, the glove puppet, and I'm going to help the children to speak.'

Celia laughed. 'So that's what you wanted all those old woollies for! What a good idea.

Will it work, do you think?'

'I hope so,' Megan said. 'I saw the idea in one of our therapy journals and I'm going to try it on some of my delayed language cases. A lot of them are too shy and withdrawn to speak to each other but they might through a puppet.' She pushed 'Henry' into her case. 'Anyway, keep your fingers crossed.'

'I'd say that the only mistake you've made is making them too attractive,' Celia said. 'They won't want to part with them at the end of the session!' She sighed. 'As far as keeping your fingers crossed goes – keep yours crossed for me, won't you? Steve is picking me up for lunch.'

Megan looked helplessly at her friend's anxious face. 'Nothing is ever as bad as you think it'll be. Try not to worry.' She patted Celia's arm, but at the same time she couldn't help thinking that she was a fine person to be giving advice of that kind!

At Brinkdown Health Centre the waiting room was crowded with small patients and their mothers. She was delighted to see that Damion Shaw was amongst them and that he was wearing his Edinborough Masker. When she asked his mother how he was getting on with it she found her surprised and thrilled by the results.

'I'd never have believed that a thing like that could work so well,' she said enthusiastically. 'When he's wearing it he doesn't stammer at all and oddly enough the other kids at school seem to be green with envy! It's become a sort of status symbol. One little boy even went as far as to say he'd rather have one of them than false teeth like his grandad's!'

Megan laughed. 'Aren't they funny? One thing about children is that they're so unpredictable. It's impossible to be bored by them! But you must remember to make Damion practice without his masker each day,' she reminded. 'We're going to have some new games today, so maybe you can carry on with them at home.'

When she had prepared the room, Megan had the delayed language patients in together as a group. As Damion was the only stammer patient she included him, feeling that he could well be a help to the others. She had pinned a large coloured picture to the wall and when the children were seated in a semicircle she handed them the glove puppets. She was rewarded by bright smiles all round as they fitted them onto their small hands.

Megan removed Damion's masker and at the same time she explained to the group what she wanted them to do:

'There are lots of things in the picture,' she said, pointing. 'And I want these little animals to have a good look and then tell each other all about it.' She held up Damion's hand which was wearing the horse puppet. 'This is Henry Horse,' she told the others. 'But the other puppets haven't got names so I want you to think of some. There are some more horses in the picture and I want Henry to tell us how many and what each of them is doing.'

To Megan's delight Damion seemed to have a real flair for the game. He made 'Henry' peer short-sightedly at the picture and when he 'spoke' it was with a personality all his own. With barely a hint of his former stammer he told the other children all about the horses in the picture, even making up names for them and he was so amusing that he had the others in fits of laughter. Encouraged by his example they began to follow suit, doing their best to ape him and at the end of the session Megan was more than pleased with the experiment. She showed the mothers how to make their own puppets from oddments at home and urged them to play the game as often as the child wanted to.

On her way to the afternoon clinic Megan passed the end of the road where Peter Forbes lived and she decided that as she had half an hour to spare she would drop in and see how he was getting along.

Mrs Forbes greeted her warmly and invited her inside. 'He's doing so well now, thanks to you, Miss Lacey,' she said. 'And guess what the latest is? He's got a job!'

'That's marvellous!' Megan smiled. 'But how did he manage it?'

'The man who runs the little filling station on the corner of the road came to see him – Peter always used to get his petrol for the bike there,' she explained. 'And he used to let Peter have the use of his workshop for tinkering and so on. Well, he asked Peter if he'd like to work there a couple of hours each evening. He's gone self-service, you see, so he only has to sit in the office and take the money.' She smiled. 'You wouldn't believe the difference it's made to him. You'll be really surprised. Come and see him.'

As usual Peter was sitting in the garden. He had acquired a healthy tan and instead of the science fiction magazine he was reading an engineering manual. He grinned cheerily when he saw Megan.

'Hello, Miss Lacey,' he said with only the

slightest hint of hesitation.

'Hello, Peter. I've been hearing all about your new job,' she told him.

Peter frowned at his mother. 'Blow! I wanted to tell her,' he said. He held out the manual to Megan and she saw that it was a plan of a motor-cycle. 'When John's hands are better we're going to build our own bike,' he told her. 'Mr Smith at the filling station says we can do it there. One day we're going to have our own factory!'

In the house after their talk Megan spoke to Mrs Forbes: 'His words are still a little slurred, but a lot less than before,' she said. 'You'll notice that he'll improve increasingly now as the time goes by. The encouraging thing is that it no longer bothers him – perhaps because his friend John has the same problem. He's got his interest in life back and now that he has something to feel enthusiastic about his speech no longer worries him.' She smiled. 'We're definitely winning, Mrs Forbes!'

It was a long day and Megan would dearly have loved to go straight home and put her feet up, but she remembered that she had to attend the meeting about the combined clinic that evening at the health centre. It wasn't worth going home and she had told

Celia that she would have something to eat out that evening. With Steve there she had thought it more tactful anyway.

She found a small Italian restaurant quite near to the centre and had a light meal, then went along to join the others who were already gathered in the lecture room. As well as herself and Jeff Maitland the team consisted of Maurice Dobbs, the consultant neurologist, a plastic surgeon and a psychologist; the School Medical Officer, head of the physiotherapy department and a teacher of the deaf. Megan found a seat and a few minutes later Jeff slid into the one beside her and began to point out the people who were so far unknown to her, telling her their names.

The meeting went well. Most of the doctors and therapists present had worked for other authorities where combined clinics had been a regular feature and most of them had interesting and constructive suggestions to contribute. Megan was asked whether she had seen many patients who, in her opinion, would benefit from the clinic and she said that she had. She had seen several baffling cases which might be passed around from doctor to doctor for months before being correctly diagnosed, whereas being seen by the team would cut out a lot of the time-consuming consultation, not to mention endless paper work.

Coffee was served after the meeting and Jeff took her round and introduced her to the people she had not yet met. She found everyone friendly and enjoyed chatting so much that she hardly noticed what the time was. Presently Jeff appeared again at her side.

'Have you eaten, Meg?'

She nodded. 'Yes. Before the meeting.'

'Then come and have a drink. I want to talk to you.'

She shook her head. 'I'm very tired. If you don't mind we'll make it some other time.'

He grasped her arm firmly. 'No. We'll make it now!'

Too weak to argue she followed him out to the car park.

'How about going to the Rose and Crown?' he said. 'That's about half way for you.'

She shrugged. 'Just as you like. I can't think why you bother to ask!'

As she followed the tail light of his car she wondered what on earth she was doing. She must be mad, letting him bulldoze her into having a drink she didn't want – not to mention the 'talk'. Why was it she found him so hard to refuse? He just wouldn't take no for an answer and he seemed as thick-skinned as a rhinoceros!

It was cosy and intimate inside the Rose and Crown and they took their drinks to the seclusion of the inglenook fireplace as they had done on that other occasion. Jeff looked at her thoughtfully.

'Well, the clinic being fixed for Thursday morning should have pleased you.'

'I shall still have some re-shuffling to do,' she said.

'Mmm – you're still looking a bit wan,' he said.

She gave him a wry look. 'Thanks! Is that what you brought me here to tell me? If so it would have done another time!'

He winced. 'Well, your claws are still sharp at any rate!' He reached out and touched her hand. 'Are you going to tell me, Megan?'

She pulled her hand away. 'Tell you what?'

'Tell me what it is that makes you lash out at me whenever we meet. You've done it right from the first. And that night when you stormed out of my flat is still a mystery to me. I think you owe me an explanation for that at least, especially after I'd just given you half my steak!'

She sighed wearily. 'Well, if I have to I

think it can best be summed up by saying that I simply don't like your type. Everything about you – everything you do, say and think goes against the grain with me. I think that when one meets a person like that one should avoid them as much as possible, don't you?'

He leaned back in his chair and opened his eyes wide. 'Well – you don't take any prisoners, do you? I know we had that brush in the car park on your first day, but surely that couldn't have been bad enough to make you hate me for ever?'

Megan took a long draught of her gin and tonic. 'It doesn't matter very much to either of us what I think, does it?' she asked. 'We work together quite amicably – soon I'll be married to David. You have heaps of friends. Why should it bother you?'

'I don't know – but nevertheless, it does.' He leaned towards her. 'And as you've brought the subject up – are you *really* going to marry David Lattimer?'

She looked up at him sharply. 'Of course, we're engaged, aren't we?'

'You may be, but you don't love him, do you?'

A stinging protest sprang to her lips but suddenly her eyes met his and she couldn't speak. To her horror she felt tears well up in her eyes and she hastily swallowed the rest of her drink in an effort to wash away the lump in her throat. Without another word he took her arm and raised her to her feet, steering her towards the door and out into the cool evening air. In the car park he stopped and handed her a large handkerchief from his pocket.

'Here, do you need this?'

She swallowed hard again. 'No – I'm fine – thanks.'

He opened the door of his car. 'Get in a minute.'

Without quite knowing why, she obeyed him. In the darkness he turned to her.

'Want to talk about it? After all, who better than a person with whom you've absolutely nothing in common?'

'It – it's so hard to explain,' she said. 'David's – well he's not who I thought he was.'

He frowned. 'You mean he's fallen short of your expectations in some way?'

'No – the opposite. He's too good and he deserves better. I don't want to hurt him and it seems inevitable that I shall, one way or the other.'

He shook his head. 'Then don't you think

that the sooner you get it over with the better?' He sighed. 'That's the trouble with getting close to people; sooner or later one of you always gets hurt.' He leaned back in his seat. 'I have a young sister, I may have mentioned her to you. We were brought up by an uncle and aunt on a sheep station in New South Wales. Debbie was almost as good as a brother and we were very close. When it was time for college we went to live in Melbourne and it was there that she met the man she finally married – who also happened to be my best friend.' He sighed. 'I've never seen two people change so much. I could hardly believe it! Neither of them wanted me any more. They became the two most boring people in the world – all wound up in each other and things like furniture and washing machines. All the fun went out of them and, consequently, out of me too. That was when I swore that I'd never make another close relationship – and as for *marriage!* You won't catch me turning into a one-track turnip-head like that!'

Megan sniffed. 'I can't say I blame you.'

He peered at her through the gloom. 'Is there anything I can do to help, Megan?'

She shook her head. 'I don't really see that there is.'

'I hate to see you looking so forlorn.' He put a finger under her chin and turned her face towards him, then he bent and kissed her, drawing her into his arms and holding her close in the darkness. Her heart seemed to miss several beats as she closed her eyes and gave herself up to his kisses. Her arms crept round his neck and for a moment she surrendered to the thrill of his vibrant strength and the insistence of his mouth against hers.

'You don't really hate me, do you, Meg?' he whispered against her hair. 'It's quite the opposite, isn't it? Why have you always fought so hard against it?' His lips found hers again this time harder, demanding her response till she pushed him angrily from her, coming at last to her senses.

'I suppose you think a girl in my position is easy prey!' she said shakily. 'Catch them when they're weak and vulnerable – is that your motto? Well, I'm sorry to disappoint you, but this time you've picked the wrong girl!' And she opened the car door and got out.

Her knees trembled as she walked across the car park and unlocked the door of her own car, but she had not had time to get in before Jeff caught her up. His hair was standing on end where he had pushed an exasperated hand through it and his eyes were steely with anger.

'Just what the hell is the matter with you?' he demanded loudly. 'One minute you're all softness, then suddenly you're tearing at me like a tigress again. I really ought to give you a damned good spanking. I've never met anyone who deserved it more!'

She rounded on him angrily. 'That's all you understand, isn't it? You're one of those men who thinks that's all a woman really needs to keep her in line. No wonder your sister was glad to see the back of you! You're about as sensitive as a – as a – *kangaroo!*' And with a twist of her ignition key she brought the car to life and roared out of the car park, satisfied that for once she had actually had the last word. But by the time she was halfway home the reaction set in. Her anger dimmed, all she could clearly remember was the feel of his lips on hers and all her most vehement inward denials could not quench the certain knowledge that she was hopelessly and help-lessly in love with Jeff Maitland.

She took her time in putting away the car, wondering whether Steve was still at the cottage with Celia, but when she put her head round the living room door she found her friend alone.

'Hello,' she said. 'I thought you might still have company.'

Celia shook her head. 'You're not going to believe this. There I was with my courage all screwed up – then Steve rang to say he had to take his mother down to Bristol. His married sister has been taken into hospital with appendicitis and someone has to go down and look after her two children.'

'What did you say?' Megan asked.

Celia shrugged. 'What can you say on the phone? Now I have to wait till Wednesday because naturally Steve will be staying over-night to see that his sister's okay. I've invited him to come here for dinner on Wednesday evening.' She glanced apologetically at Megan. 'Would you mind very much if I asked you to make yourself scarce that night?'

'Of course not. I'll stay over in Kingscroft and have a bite to eat with Jane,' Megan said. 'She'll probably be quite glad of the company.'

When she suggested it to her on Wednesday afternoon at the hospital, Jane was glad of the prospect of company.

'I had my notification this morning,' she confided. 'I'm to go into Brinkdown General two weeks from today and I don't mind admitting that I've got a bad case of the jitters.'

Megan gave her arm a squeeze. 'Maybe we'll have time for a film or something when we've eaten. That would help to take your mind off things.'

Jane's face brightened. 'Sounds great. I'll borrow a local paper and find out what's on.'

On her way to her room Megan passed Jeff in the corridor. He nodded curtly and passed on without a word. Closing the door of her room firmly, she closed her eyes. If only she could get the wretched man out of her hair!

The girls ate a snack meal at Jane's flat and then went into Kingscroft's one and only cinema where a popular comedy thriller was being shown. They arrived just as the lights were going down but as the film began they were disturbed by two latecomers. Megan stood up to allow them to pass. She raised her eyes and to her horror, found herself looking straight into those of Jeff Maitland. His companion was Julia Simms. What made it even worse was that the only vacant seats in the row were right next to her and a moment later she found Jeff actually sitting in the next seat.

She never really knew what the film was about. Concentration was impossible. All she was aware of was Jeff's presence. She could actually feel the warmth of his arm through her sleeve. She did notice however, that his arm was draped casually round Julia's shoulders and that they seemed happy and relaxed together. From time to time she heard them laugh at something in the film, she heard Jeff's voice speaking quietly – too quietly for her to hear the actual words – then Julia's responses – equally quiet. Once she stole a look in their direction and saw that Julia was looking up at Jeff with glowing eyes. Her heart twisted painfully as she looked quickly away.

The moment the film was over she stood up, eager to get away from Jeff and the cinema as soon as possible. But just as they were moving into the aisle Jane noticed Jeff and exclaimed with delight:

'Jeff! Don't tell me you've been sitting there all evening without us knowing!'

He grinned, not looking at Megan. 'Looks like it. Did you enjoy the film?'

'Oh, very much, didn't we, Megan?'

Megan muttered non-committally and Jane went on:

'By the way, I heard this morning that I'm

to have my op' two weeks from tomorrow.'

He nodded. 'That's great.'

'Will you be there?' she asked.

'I shall be assisting,' he told her. 'I'm looking forward to seeing Mr Oldershaw operate. He's supposed to be the best in the country.'

Jane smiled. 'Well, that's encouraging, though I can't exactly say that I'm looking forward to it!'

Megan's jaws ached with the effort of maintaining her smile. She tried to make small-talk with Julia, but found her unresponsive and slightly hostile. Maybe she had seen Megan looking at her while the film was on and thought she had been spying. The thought made her go hot with embarrassment. At last Jane's conversation with Jeff came to an end and they all moved towards the cinema exit. Outside Jeff and Julia went off to the car park and Jane looked at Megan.

'Coming back to the flat for coffee?'

Megan looked at her watch. 'Why not? I'll have to come back to collect the car anyway and it's still quite early.'

Jane made coffee in the trim little kitchen and Megan noticed that she seemed quite cheerful again. Ironically, it was she who had hit the depths this time, but she was determined that Jane should not notice it. She looked around the room and noticed a photograph of Jane with a good-looking young man.

'Who's this?' she asked as the other girl came in with the tray. 'Boy friend? He's very good-looking.'

Jane's face fell as she put the tray down on the table. 'He is nice, isn't he? He hasn't been around much lately though, like so many of my other friends. I know I haven't been very good company but I must say that I thought Richard would have been – well, at least more sympathetic.'

'Have you known him long?' Megan asked.

Jane nodded. 'Since ever really. We grew up together. Oh, there was a long period when we didn't see one another, when he was away at university, then we met again and started going out together. I thought at one time it might get to be quite serious, but then–' she shrugged. 'Maybe he just didn't fancy having an invalid on his hands.'

In spite of her light tone, Megan could see that Jane was really hurt by Richard's rejection. 'If that's really what he thought then maybe you're better off without him,' she said gently. But it was clear that Jane didn't think so. 'Does he live in Kingscroft?' she asked.

Jane shook her head. 'Brinkdown. He teaches at the Grammar School there. You may have seen him playing in the cricket match against the hospital the other week. He teaches classics but he's a keen sportsman too. As a matter of fact he's quite friendly with Jeff Maitland. They often play squash together.'

'Didn't he give any reason for dropping your relationship?' Megan asked. But again, Jane shook her head.

'No. He just let it fizzle out.' She looked up at Megan with an expression of apprehension. 'Megan – I know I shouldn't but I've been reading up about this operation and I'm scared stiff. When I go in – will you come with me – just for moral support?'

Megan clicked her tongue. 'You know as well as I do that "reading up" is the worst thing you can do. You'll be fine. You're going to be in the very best hands, Jeff's seen to that for you. You really must stop letting your imagination run wild.'

'But you have to admit it is tricky,' Jane said biting her lip. 'And accidents have been known–'

'There'll be no accident!' Megan said

firmly. 'And as for coming in with you, of course I will. As it happens I'm in Brinkdown all day on Thursdays, so I'll be able to keep looking in on you between clinics. How's that?'

The other girl smiled, giving a sigh of relief. 'You really are a friend Megan and it's true what they say: it takes trouble to find out who your real ones are.'

As she put the car away, Megan noticed that a light still burned in the living room of the cottage. She wondered if Steve was still there. But she didn't have to wonder for long. She was just about to grasp the handle of the front door when it was jerked out of her hand as the door flew open abruptly. A very angry-looking young man strode past her, almost knocking her over. He mumbled a graceless apology and a moment later had disappeared into the night. Celia stood in the hall, looking pale and shaken. Megan closed the door behind her and looked at her friend.

'Well – I take it that was Steve.'

'Yes – sorry I couldn't introduce you.' Celia lifted her shoulders. 'Come into the kitchen while I make some coffee. I feel I need some.'

Megan looked at her white face. 'He took

it badly then?'

'Just about as badly as it's possible,' Celia told her. 'He accused me of two-timing him with David – well, I'd guessed he would. It didn't make any difference when I told him that David was engaged to you either. In fact he didn't even seem to believe in your existence! That's why I was glad you arrived just as he was leaving.'

Megan took the cup of coffee that Celia handed her. 'So it's over?'

Celia sighed. 'Yes – but I'd rather we'd parted on better terms.' She sat at the table, her shoulders slumped as she stirred her coffee.

'Aren't you relieved though?' Megan asked.

She lifted her shoulders in a helpless gesture. 'I just feel depressed. It all seems such a waste of time and emotion and – oh, *everything!*' Tears filled her eyes and Megan touched her arm.

'Go on – up to bed. I'll bring you a couple of aspirins. Things always look much better in the morning.'

As she washed up the cups at the sink and tidied the kitchen she couldn't help thinking of her own ordeal. She had been putting it off, but she must see David soon and tell him she couldn't marry him. What a trio they were, Celia, Jane and she. Maybe Jeff had the best idea after all; maybe it *was* better not to develop close relationships. How did one avoid it though? That was the question. Standing at the window she let her mind drift back to Jeff again. His disturbing presence in the cinema this evening; the sound of his voice, the pure strength of him that could make for such warmth and security but only made her feel weak and vulnerable. Tiredness dragged at her limbs as she went upstairs to her room and by the time she climbed into bed she had made a decision: after she had broken with David – when Jane was fully recovered and didn't need her any more, she would look for another job that was as far away from the Cotswolds and Jeff Maitland as she could get! Only then would she know peace again.

CHAPTER EIGHT

At the other end of the line the telephone rang on and on. Megan stared at the receiver in her hand. Surely David must be at home at this time on a Monday morning. Why was it that something always stopped her just when she had made her mind up?

She had had all weekend to think about it. David had been away on a weekend conference in Derbyshire. Last night she had gone over and over what she would say and as soon as she woke this morning she had decided to ring him and arrange for them to meet – now there was no reply. Puzzled, she shook her head. He was due home last night. She hung up and dialled the number of the surgery where he might have gone in early for some reason. But the voice that answered was unfamiliar to her:

'Good morning. Can I help you?'

'Oh – good morning. I was trying to contact Doctor Lattimer,' Megan said hesitantly. 'It's Megan Lacey, his fiancée.'

'Oh yes, Miss Lacey. David left a message

for you. I'm afraid he was called away in the early hours of this morning. It's his grandfather down in Hampshire. He's been ailing for some time and it appears that he's taken a turn for the worse and has been asking for David. He left at about five-thirty and rang to ask my husband, Doctor Banks, to hold the fort for a few days. I suppose he didn't want to disturb you at that time of the morning.'

'I see. Thank you, Mrs Banks,' Megan said. 'I suppose I shall be hearing from him. Goodbye.'

Wearily, she replaced the receiver. Fate seemed determined to hold her up each time she tried to break off their engagement. Like Celia she had summoned up all of her courage only to be let down again. She checked herself, biting her lip. How could she have such thoughts when a poor old man was ill, probably dying? David would be so upset. As far as she knew his grandfather was his only surviving relative – yet here she was thinking of herself again!

She went into the kitchen and put the kettle on. She would take Celia a cup of tea in bed as a treat – and to prove to herself that she wasn't really selfish!

Celia was already awake but she was glad

of the tea.

'Thanks. You really are spoiling me,' she said, sitting up in bed. Megan told her about the call she'd just made and the news Mrs Banks had given her and Celia drank her tea down hurriedly and got out of bed.

'I'd better get down to the surgery early and put a call through to Doctor Banks myself,' she said. 'Maybe David will have left me some instructions.' She looked at Megan, suddenly struck by a thought. 'Why were you ringing him so early? Did you want him for something important? If he rings during the day while I'm at the surgery can I give him a message – tell him to ring you?'

But Megan shook her head. 'No – it was nothing really,' she said feebly. 'I just happened to be awake early so I thought I'd ring him.'

Celia gave her a wistful look. 'Mmm – I know the feeling.'

Something in her tone made Megan look at her. There was a far away look in her eyes. She obviously thought that Megan was so much in love that she'd wanted to hear David's voice as soon as she woke! If only she knew the truth, Megan thought guiltily.

When she arrived home that evening she found Celia in the kitchen. It seemed that

David had rung during the afternoon. His grandfather had died at midday, just after he arrived at the hospital, but he would have to stay on for a few days to arrange the funeral and contact all the old man's friends.

'Poor David, he sounded so tired. He can hardly have had any sleep and then that long drive–' She broke off and turned away, but not before Megan had seen the flush in her cheeks. For the first time she was struck by a thought: was Celia more than just fond of David herself? She had vehemently denied it when Steve had accused her. Perhaps it was possible that she had not realised it herself until recently. They had known each other for a long time – and worked closely together. Megan groaned inwardly. More complications!

With the commencement of the new combined clinic, Megan found it necessary to reshuffle her work schedule a little and the following day she decided to call on Mrs Slater and her daughter. She found them doing the housework together; Mrs Slater dusting from her wheelchair, while Mrs Smith vacuumed the carpets. It seemed that the day centre and occupational therapy were working out well. Mrs Slater enjoyed the change of scene and the company, whilst her daughter used the time to catch up on her chores or, as she cheerfully told Megan:

'Now that I've roped Mother in for some of the jobs I even have time to pop down the road for a coffee and a chat with my friend!'

Megan looked at them both. They seemed happier and more relaxed with each other and as Mrs Smith saw her out she confided that this was so.

'She isn't half as depressed since she started at the day centre,' she said. 'They let her do a little cooking there and her hands are so much better she can even do her knitting again. Do you know, I really think she might be able to go home again eventually.' She smiled. 'I never thought that a month ago. Thanks a lot for getting her in at the centre, Miss Lacey. They've really given her back her independence.'

Megan nodded. 'I've a feeling that the day centre is only a small contributing factor in her recovery,' she said. 'Your faith in her and your encouragement have really done the trick.'

Mrs Smith coloured. 'I feel ashamed when I think of the way I was treating her – as though she was finished and useless,' she said. 'It was just that I didn't understand till you talked to me. We get on so well together

189

now, just like in the old days. I shall really miss her when she's well enough to go home.'

Wednesday came and also the clinic at Kingscroft. Megan avoided Jeff altogether. After the episode in the cinema she felt she simply couldn't face him. She spent the evening with Jane at her flat, relaxing and exchanging news.

'It's the hospital dance on Saturday,' Jane told her. 'One of the physios at Brinkdown rang me today and asked me if I'd take some tickets. Do you want to go?'

'I don't know whether David will be home in time,' Megan said. 'And even if he is he might not feel like it after his grandfather's death.

'No, I suppose not. I won't be going either this year,' Jane said wistfully. 'I have no one to go with.' She grinned. 'We shall have to go together like two old maids!'

On Thursday morning she was at Brinkdown General in plenty of time for the first of the combined clinics. She was quite looking forward to it as she had several patients whom she had recommended herself, one of whom was a little girl of five with severe delayed language problems for which there seemed no physical cause. The only thing that spoiled her anticipation was that there was little hope of avoiding Jeff under the circumstances. She would just have to hope that they were kept too busy for them to exchange any conversation of a personal nature.

The group of doctors and therapists settled down to observe the patients being interviewed on the other side of the two-way mirror, microphones enabling them to hear their voices and the answers to the questions they were asked. The morning passed quickly and after the last patient had been seen several of the doctors most concerned stayed on to discuss what they had seen.

At last she got away and, looking at her watch, decided that she just had time for a quick lunch in the canteen before going on to the Health Centre for her clinic there which had been shifted to the afternoon. As she threaded her way between the crowded tables looking for somewhere to sit, she heard a familiar voice hailing her:

'Hi, Meg! There's a free seat here. Come and join us.'

She hesitated. The very last person she wanted to sit with was Jeff, but it seemed she had no choice. Besides, there was someone with him – another man, so perhaps it wouldn't be too embarrassing. Her face pink, she put her tray down and slid into the vacant chair.

He looked at her tray. 'Good lord! How do you manage to keep a figure like yours on stuff like that?'

To her annoyance she felt her colour deepen. 'I don't often eat egg and chips but I'm hungry and I have a busy afternoon in front of me. Anyway, what has it to do with you what I eat?'

He winced and grinned across the table to his companion. 'Ouch! Told you she was a regular tiger, didn't I?' He laughed. 'Megan, this is Richard Neale. You'll remember him. He was the chap who caught me out so unsportingly at the cricket match. He teaches at the local seat of learning.'

Megan looked up with interest. This must be the young man in the photograph with Jane. Yes, he was even more good-looking in the flesh. She smiled and held out her hand. 'How do you do. I'm Megan Lacey.'

He shook her hand. 'I know, Jeff has been telling me about you.'

She glanced at Jeff, wondering just *what* he had been saying about her.

Richard Neale stood up. 'I'm afraid I shall have to be going now. Nice to have met you,

Megan. See you later, Jeff.'

When he had gone Jeff grinned. 'Good bloke, Richard. He popped over to ask me to play squash with him at the school courts this evening.'

'He may be a "good bloke" but I don't think that what he did to Jane was very nice,' Megan said tucking into her egg and chips.

Jeff raised an eyebrow. 'Did to Jane. What did he do?'

'They were going out together – till he knew she was going into hospital, then he just dropped her.' She glanced up at him. 'But then I suppose you'd approve of that kind of treatment!'

But he was frowning. 'Look, Megan – I only said I didn't believe in marriage or close relationships *myself*. I don't go around encouraging other people to hurt one another. It's just my personal opinion. Understand?'

She shrugged. 'I couldn't care less about your personal opinions, but I do care about Jane. She's a nice girl and she needs her friends at a time like this.'

He leaned his arms on the table. 'I agree wholeheartedly. But it just doesn't sound like Richard. Tell me more. What happened?'

She shook her head. 'All I know is that the

relationship just fizzled out and that she misses him. Apparently it had been going on for quite some time.'

Again Jeff frowned. 'I know it had. Look, leave it with me, will you? If Richard will talk to anyone it'll be me. I'll get to the bottom of it. I wouldn't have little Jane hurt for the world.'

She looked at him, one eyebrow raised ironically. 'Another of the league of Maitland girlfriends, eh?'

He nodded. 'She's a mate – yes.'

Megan made an attempt at a sardonic laugh but it was completely lost on him as he waved to a group of nurses across the room. She was just pushing her plate away when he asked her:

'Are you coming to the hospital dance on Saturday?'

'I doubt it,' she told him. 'David has been away. His grandfather has died. Even if he gets back in time he probably won't feel like going.'

'Go with me then.'

She stared at him. 'I shall pretend you didn't say that – for your sake!'

He assumed an innocent look. 'Why, for heaven's sake? I'm only asking you to a dance – not to elope! Anyway, I thought you were going to break this ridiculous engagement thing off.'

She stood up. 'I do still have some feeling for others though, which is more than I can say for you!' And turning, she walked purposely towards the door.

He caught up with her in the corridor. 'Listen, Meg, I'm sorry. I wasn't thinking what I was saying. 'Look, take these two tickets in case David does get back in time. You needn't pay for them if you don't use them.' He pushed the tickets into her pocket and for a moment his eyes held hers. 'I wish I could get you out of my system, Meg,' he said quietly.

Her heart jumped painfully. 'You make me sound like an attack of measles or something,' she said shakily.

He shook his head. 'Oh no. I've had measles and believe me, it's nothing by comparison.' He leaned one hand on the wall behind her and looked into her eyes. 'Come out with me tonight, Meg?' he asked.

She ducked out from under his arm deftly. 'No thanks. Get yourself immunised somewhere else!' she said as she hurried away.

In the car park she unlocked the car and got in, but before she could turn the ignition key he had caught her up and was tapping on her window. Embarrassed, she wound the window down and he bent to look in at her.

'Why is it that most of our conversations are conducted in car parks?' Without waiting for her to answer he went on: 'I'll tell you why, shall I? It's because you're always running away from me. You're afraid! That's it, isn't it?' he persisted.

She took a deep breath. 'Look, I have a clinic at the Health Centre. I shall be late if you don't let me go.'

He ignored her. 'Your trouble is that you're afraid of your own emotions. I've never seen anyone as inhibited as you. Yet I know you can be warm when you let yourself go.' He reached into the car to touch her shoulder. 'I've had one or two glimpses of the real Megan Lacey and it made me want to see more. Let yourself go and start living, Meg.'

She pushed his hand away. 'Stop calling me Meg, I don't like it!' she exploded. 'There's only one person who ever calls me Meg. And as for all that other rubbish – I've never heard of anything so downright stupid. You're a conceited, self-centred bore, Jeff Maitland, and when I do "start living" as you call it it will be with someone worthwhile – and as far away from *you* as I can get!' And she drove away, leaving him staring after her.

It wasn't until she was halfway to the Health Centre that she realised something else too – he had been right: she *was* afraid! She knew that if she gave full rein to her feelings for Jeff she'd be hurt as she'd never been hurt in her life before – and she didn't relish the prospect.

That evening when she got home she found David in the kitchen talking to Celia. He greeted her warmly.

'It's good to be home. The funeral was this morning but I didn't want to hang around after it was over. Poor Jim Banks must have been snowed under. Celia tells me that the kids have started their usual crop of summer ailments – chicken pox and mumps!'

'I've asked David to stay and eat with us,' Celia said. 'There's plenty for three and Mrs Jenkins doesn't know he's home yet.'

'Of course,' Megan agreed. She looked at Celia's flushed face and the thought she'd had earlier in the week crept back again. She noticed that Celia avoided looking at David but that when she did the expression in her eyes was unmistakable. Megan sighed inwardly. Poor Celia. What a mess.

They sat down to eat and David asked

about what had been happening in the village during his absence. The conversation was mainly between him and Celia as she was the one who had taken all his calls. It occurred to Megan that Celia would make him an ideal wife – much better than she would. Why couldn't people ever seem to fall in love with those best suited to them?

'I've a bit of news that will surprise you,' David said. 'My grandfather has left me his practice down in the West Country. Although the old chap was over eighty he had been struggling along until his illness, apparently because he wanted to keep the practice for me, bless his old heart. At the moment there's a locum in charge. So I'm faced with the decision either to sell up and stay on here, or go down and start building it up again. Since the old chap's illness things have slipped a little.' He looked at Megan. 'The choice is yours, really.'

She felt her colour rise. Looking across the table she saw the look of misery on Celia's face. 'Oh no!' she said. 'I couldn't think of trying to influence you, David. You must decide.'

He sighed. 'It's beautiful country, on the edge of the New Forest and of course there's the house too; a lovely old thatched farmhouse. He always wanted me to have it so much – and yet I shall hate leaving here.' He looked at Megan. 'Your work is here too. I haven't forgotten that. It wouldn't be fair to expect you to give it up.'

She shook her head. 'Let's not talk about it now. You must be tired.'

'I am, rather.' He looked at his watch. 'I must go over and see Jim Banks this evening too. Thanks for the meal, girls. I'll see you both tomorrow.'

They both went to the door with him and waved him off, then they returned to the kitchen where Megan started to clear the table.

'I'll wash up as you cooked the meal,' she said. 'Why don't you go and watch T.V. I'll bring you some coffee when I've finished.'

But Celia shook her head. 'No, we'll do it together as we always do. Then we can both sit down.'

For a while they worked in silence, Megan busy with her own thoughts, then she decided to take the bull by the horns.

'Celia,' she said. 'When you decided that you weren't in love with Steve any longer – was it because there was – someone else? I know Steve upset you when he accused you of being in love with David, but might there have been a grain of truth in what he thought?'

Celia put down the plate she was drying and bit her lip.

'I'm sorry, Megan. I didn't mean you to know – ever – either of you. I'd have given anything in the world for it not to have happened but I just couldn't help myself.' She looked at Megan. 'I'm sure it's only on my side though, so don't worry. It's a good thing you'll be going away – and when I don't see him any more I'll–' She broke off, tears filling her eyes and Megan touched her arm.

'Don't get upset, Celia, please. It will work out – you'll see. Look, I'm not saying anything now, but just leave it to me and have faith, will you? I've been doing a lot of thinking lately and I've got a hunch.'

'What do you mean? What are you going to do?' Celia looked alarmed. But Megan just smiled.

'Wait and see.'

When she reached Grey's Lodge a light was still burning downstairs and she heaved a sigh of relief. She had been afraid David might have turned in early and if she had had to put it off again she would not have slept a wink. She rang the bell, hoping that David wouldn't be too disturbed, he really must be longing for a good night's sleep himself.

He answered the door almost immediately and seeing that it was Megan he smiled with relief.

'Jim Banks did say he'd take my night calls for tonight, but there's always the odd patient who comes to the door. I must say I'm relieved it's you.' He held the door open for her and she went past him into the hall.

'I won't take up too much of your time, David,' she said. As they went through to the pleasant sitting room at the back of the house her knees were shaking. Suppose that what she had worked out in her mind were just wishful thinking after all? Suppose she was about to make yet another mistake? But whatever came out of it one thing was certain: she must tell David that she couldn't marry him – and tell him now.

He closed the door and looked at her. 'Is anything wrong, Megan?'

She shook her head. 'No – well, yes, in a way.'

He smiled. 'Well at least sit down. Would you like anything – coffee or a sherry perhaps?'

'No – nothing thank you. I'd rather come straight to the point.' She took a deep breath.

'I don't believe that our being engaged is right. I – I believe that your true feelings are with someone else – but that you're letting chivalry prevent you from speaking out.' She let her breath out on a sigh and sank slowly into a chair. There! She had actually said it – at last!

David's face had paled and he felt for a chair and sat down himself. 'What makes you say this, Megan?'

She smiled. 'Call it a hunch if you like. I get them from time to time and they're hardly ever wrong. I believe you've loved Celia ever since she first came to work for you two years ago. Steve saw it and that was why he made her leave. You never said anything to her because she was engaged to someone else. What you don't know is that Celia has realised her mistake now and she's very unhappy.' She leaned towards him. 'Please tell me the truth, David. I'm right, aren't I? We made a mistake and we have to put it right before it's too late.'

He went to the dresser and took out a bottle of brandy, pouring himself a large measure. 'I need this,' he told her. 'What about you? I think you must need one too!'

She nodded gratefully and he poured a glass and brought it to her. 'Well,' he said, looking down at her, 'all that took quite a bit of courage, not to say an acute perception.'

She sipped the searing liquid with relief. 'You haven't told me yet – I'm right, aren't I?'

He nodded. 'I feel I owe you an apology. I really thought I was over Celia. As you said, I'd never spoken to her about the way I felt because she was already engaged and, as far as I knew, happy about it. You came to the village and when I met you I thought you were my ideal girl.' He smiled. 'I still think you're pretty terrific! But then Celia came back to work for me again. When I offered her the job I thought I was proving something to myself. But I was wrong. I sensed that her engagement was shaky and it was enough to awaken all the old feelings.' He shook his head. 'I don't mind admitting I've had very little peace since, trying to sort out my tangled feelings.'

Megan laughed. 'Well now it's all over. You're free – as from this moment.' She drew off David's ring and held it out to him.

He grinned at her wryly as he took it. 'At the risk of seeming to want to have my cake and eat it I have to say that your eagerness to break off our engagement is not very flattering!'

She coloured. 'Oh! I'm sorry, David. I *am* fond of you, I hope the three of us will always be friends, but to be absolutely honest it was never really love, was it? Celia will make you a marvellous wife, far better than I ever would.'

He looked at her, his head on one side. 'And just who is it you've set *your* sights on?'

'Does there have to be someone?' she asked defensively.

He nodded. 'I think so. For you to be so sure that what you felt for me wasn't the real thing you must have found it. Are you going to tell me who the lucky fellow is as we're being so straight with each other?'

Megan shook her head. 'It isn't that straightforward. In my case there'll be no happy ending. In fact I may soon be moving right away from here.' She handed him her empty glass. 'I'd better go now. I take it you'll be coming round to see Celia in the near future. When you do I shall make myself scarce. Oh!' She unzipped her handbag and took out the tickets that Jeff had given her. 'Why not take her to the hospital dance on Saturday? I can't think of a more romantic setting for a proposal, can you?'

He took the tickets from her and searched her face anxiously. 'Megan – what about you? I can't accept happiness at your expense. Is there anything I can do?'

She smiled. 'No. But thank you for asking.' She stood on tiptoe and kissed his cheek. 'I'll tell you one thing: I wish it had been right for us. I think you're quite the nicest man I've ever known.'

As she walked home the first stars were twinkling in the sky and a nightingale could be heard trilling away in the vicarage trees. A wave of nostalgia engulfed her. What a perfect night for a happy ending – she couldn't help wishing just a little that it could have been hers.

CHAPTER NINE

When Megan walked into the living room of the cottage on her return from Grey's Lodge Celia looked up apprehensively.

'You haven't been long. Is – is everything all right?' she asked haltingly.

Megan smiled. 'Everything is just fine. David and I are no longer engaged and you'll be glad to know that the decision was mutual and we're both very happy about it.'

Celia bit her lip. 'Oh, Megan, I feel terrible about it. What – what did David say?'

'I think I'd better leave him to tell you himself what his feelings are.' Megan sat down on the settee. 'I feel I owe you an explanation, Celia. I did something very wrong; I encouraged David to be attracted to me but I didn't realise that he was on the rebound at the time. I mistook him for someone else, you see.'

Celia looked completely mystified and Megan laughed. 'Poor Celia. I am confusing you, aren't I? I'd better start from the beginning.' She went on to tell her about Caroline, their life together and the way she had always been over-protective, Caroline's job here in Little Avedon and, finally, the unhappy love affair she had come to avenge. By the time she had finished Celia was staring at her, her eyes wide with amazement.

'You actually got engaged to a man – just to get your own back on him? Oh, Megan! That doesn't sound like you at all!'

Megan blushed. 'I can hardly believe it myself now when I look back.' She took a deep breath. 'You know, I've developed a lot as a person since I came here – since I stopped living my life through Caroline, I suppose you could say. You see, I never allowed myself to get to know people properly; I saw things and people in terms of black and white and I simply didn't foresee the complications that could arise when one really grew to know and like a person as I grew to know and like David. It worried me terribly when I saw the mess I'd got myself into – that I might have to hurt him. I can't tell you how relieved I am that things have worked out the way they have.'

Celia looked at her enquiringly. 'And Jeff Maitland – have you any plans for chastening him?'

Megan turned away so that Celia should

not see the quick flush that crept up her face. 'I hardly think that would be possible,' she muttered.

Celia bent forward to look at her. 'Megan – oh, Megan, love, don't say you've fallen for him – not Jeff?'

Megan shook her head vigorously. 'What an idea! Of course I–' But she broke off as she met Celia's eyes. There was no deceiving her. The other girl's face showed clearly that she recognised the symptoms.

'What are you going to do about it?' she asked gently.

Megan shrugged. 'Move right away from here. I'd already decided to. I'll see Jane through her operation and then I'll give in my notice. It would only be an embarrassment to you and David to have me around anyway.'

Celia touched her arm. 'That's nonsense and you know it. What about Jeff though? I've always thought he seemed quite keen on you.'

'Oh yes – *keen*,' Megan said with a wry laugh. 'He'd no doubt be willing to include me in his collection, but a casual affair is not my scene – especially not with Jeff.' She bit her lip. 'I didn't know it was possible to feel like this,' she said in a whisper. 'I never realised how much loving a person could hurt.' She swallowed hard. 'I shall be glad when I'm away – when I can begin to forget him.'

Celia put her arm round her shoulders. 'I don't know what to say,' she said. 'Except that I do know how much it hurts. If there's anything I can do – anything at all, you know you have only to say.'

Megan smiled. 'I know, Celia. I've found good friends here, better than I deserve and I shall be really sorry to say goodbye to them all. It serves me right that I got caught in my own trap, I suppose. It's what you could call poetic justice.' She patted Celia's arm. 'Don't worry about me. I'll get over Jeff in time. And as for him, it'll be a case of out of sight – out of mind!'

The noble feeling that Megan felt at the bringing together of Celia and David was short-lived. Even the wave of relief at breaking her engagement didn't last as Friday came and went. It turned out to be 'one of those days'. First she had a puncture on the way to work, then some notes went missing and she was delayed at the clinic, keeping patients waiting long after their appointment times, which she hated. Because of this she was forced to go without her lunch and then, during the afternoon she cut her finger badly whilst sharpening a pencil. Molly Edwards, the kindly headmistress of St Angela's school for the handicapped, attended to it in her study. She looked closely at Megan as she applied a plaster from the first-aid box.

'Are you sure you're all right, Megan?' she asked. 'You're not looking yourself at all today. Maybe you need your holiday. Have you one booked?'

Megan shook her head. 'Not this year. I'm fine really. I expect it's just the shock.'

Mrs Edwards looked at her watch. 'If I were you I'd cut along home and call it a day. It's almost time anyway. The children won't mind, especially when I tell them you're poorly.' She smiled. 'They're really very fond of you, you know. They look forward to Friday afternoons all week. It's so long since we had a speech therapist and you've done so much good since you've been here.'

But her words only depressed Megan even more. She had to face the fact that her leaving would upset a lot of people, not least the patients, many of whom she had become very fond. She managed a smile.

'It's very good of you to say so, Mrs

Edwards, but I'm sure any therapist could do what I've done. Maybe I'll take your advice and go home now. Tell the children I'll make up the time with them next week.'

As soon as she let herself into the cottage she heard Celia singing, something she had not heard for some time. Slowly, she went upstairs and found her in the bedroom, trying on a new dress. When she turned to look at Megan her eyes were shining and Megan guessed at once that she and David had made their feelings known to each other.

The new dress was in a soft lilac shade which brought out the colour of Celia's eyes. There was an incandescence about her that tugged at Megan's heart. She reached out and grasped her hands, finding them cool and slightly trembling.

'You look quite lovely – and you don't have to tell me what's been happening today. Are congratulations in order?'

Celia hugged her. 'Thanks to you, yes, they are. Though of course we're keeping it very quiet for the time being. It would look rather strange to people who don't know the circumstances, wouldn't it? And one can't go round explaining.'

Megan nodded. 'You have a point there.

Still, no doubt the two of you will be going off to the West Country soon to make a new life for yourselves?'

'That is what we've decided,' Celia said happily. She peered at Megan anxiously. 'Are you all right? You're home early and you're very pale. Oh! What have you done to your finger?' She picked up the hand with the plaster and looked into Megan's face.

'It's nothing much. Just a scratch,' Megan said lightly. 'Maybe it'll teach me not to sharpen pencils with a razor blade! I take it David is taking you out?'

'Yes.' Celia frowned and bit her lip. 'You're very welcome to come along too, Megan. I don't like leaving you here on your own. I'm still not convinced about that finger. David could look at it for you.'

But Megan shook her head. 'It's fine, really. As for coming with you – I'd be about as welcome as a skeleton at a feast! You go and enjoy yourselves. I've got loads of paper-work to catch up with from last week.'

Celia sat down on the bed, her eyes dreamy. 'Oh, Megan, I still can't quite believe that David loves me. To think that I might have married Steve and never known. David would never have said anything because he thought it was all on his side.'

213

'And he might have married *me!*' Megan said with a shiver. 'I could have ruined four lives with my stupidity. Thank God I came to my senses in time.' She smiled at Celia. 'I'm so glad that you're happy – both of you.'

But when they had gone out and she sat at the table with her work spread out in front of her a feeling of desolation washed over her. The sooner she started making a new life of her own the better! When she had said that she had 'come to her senses' it was hardly true. She had only realised that she couldn't marry David when she had fallen in love with Jeff. And that was about as sensible as jumping off the roof!

The following morning she had a telephone call from Jane.

'I thought I might have heard from you. Are we going to the hospital dance tonight?' she asked.

Megan hesitated. She had quite forgotten the dance. If she went with Jane and David was there with Celia wouldn't it set tongues wagging? 'The dance–' she said. 'I– I don't know what to say. You see, something has come up.'

But Celia, who was in the kitchen and had heard the conversation, put her head round the door. 'It's all right,' she said. 'We're all going together in a party. You and Jane must come too.'

So Megan agreed. 'It's all right, I'll come. I'll pick you up at the flat at about nine o'clock,' she said.

Jane had sounded mystified as she hung up and as Megan felt she owed her an explanation she left early for Kingscroft that evening. When she got to Jane's flat she found her putting the finishing touches to her make-up in the bedroom. Megan sat on the edge of the bed.

'I've come early because I have something to tell you,' she began. 'David and I are no longer engaged. We decided to call it off mutually a couple of nights ago.'

Jane put down her lipstick and looked at Megan through the mirror. 'Well – I'll admit now that I rather suspected it wouldn't work,' she said. 'Somehow I could never quite believe that you were in love with him. What was it – rebound – an impulse thing?'

Megan nodded. 'In a way. It's a long story and one I don't come out of very well. I'll tell you all about it one day. It was on the rebound for David. I discovered that he'd been nursing a secret love for Celia for ages, but wouldn't speak out because of Steve.

Now that's over there's nothing to stop them, so there's your happy ending!'

Jane had continued to look at Megan through the mirror all this time, now she swung round on the dressing table stool and faced her. 'And you – where does your happy ending lie?'

'I shall have to wait and see, shan't I?' Megan smiled. She stood up and picked up Jane's coat. 'Come on. This evening we're going to enjoy ourselves. This time next week your operation will be over and as for me – well, I'm a free woman again, aren't I?'

But as they went out to the car Jane wasn't deceived by the lightness of Megan's tone. She knew her too well by now not to see the wistful longing in the depths of the brown eyes.

The canteen at Brinkdown General had been specially decorated for the occasion and looked very festive with its floral arrangements and candlelit tables. Megan and Jane joined David and Celia who had by now gathered the rest of the party together. There was Sister McNab and her husband, Doctor Jim Banks and his wife, Vera and two of the other secretaries from Kingscroft Cottage Hospital with their escorts. As they settled themselves at the table the floor was full of dancers and Megan found herself looking for Jeff Maitland among them. After a few moments she caught sight of him dancing with Julia Simms. They looked as though they were enjoying themselves. She looked away quickly before they could see her watching them, remembering the things she had said to him at their last meeting: 'You're a conceited, self-centred bore, Jeff Maitland!' All said because she was afraid that her feelings would show. *She* wasn't going to be just another of his conquests – she would rather be nothing at all to him! But all the self-persuasion in the world wouldn't erase the ache in her heart.

David came back from the bar with a tray of drinks and placed a glass in front of her, touching her shoulder.

'Sherry – is that all right, Megan?'

She smiled up at him. 'Fine thanks, David.' She put out her hand. 'I just wanted to say that I'm really happy for you and Celia.'

He smiled back. 'I can hardly believe it yet. If it hadn't been for you it might never have happened.'

She shook her head. 'Don't! I can't bear to think of it.'

She sipped her drink and watched as he

took to the floor with Celia, then suddenly she felt a light touch on her shoulder and turned to find herself looking into Jeff's blue eyes.

'Will you dance with me, Miss Lacey?' His eyes twinkled down at her mischievously. She began to shake her head but he raised her to her feet, one hand under her elbow in the characteristically insistent way he had. It would have been impossible to refuse without drawing attention to herself.

They stepped onto the floor and his arm encircled her waist. 'I had to talk to you, Megan,' he said. 'I know you're no fan of mine, but it's something that was bothering you and I thought you'd want to know.'

She looked up at him. 'What is it?'

'You were complaining about Richard Neale's treatment of Jane the other day and I promised to do what I could about it – right?'

She nodded. 'Did you manage to find out what the reason was?' she asked.

'I certainly did and I found out that *I* was largely to blame!' He glanced round. 'Look – come out onto the balcony. I can't explain in here, it's too noisy.'

She felt the familiar panic beginning inside her. 'Oh – er – what about Julia?' she asked.

He raised an eyebrow. 'You're always asking me that. Well – what *about* Julia?'

'Isn't she with you?'

He shook his head. 'No. She's with her new boy friend. He's an auctioneer called Bill Atkinson. That's him she's dancing with now.' He took her hand in a firm grip and led her across the room towards the door. 'There's the most marvellous view of the gasworks in the moonlight,' he said, tucking her hand through his arm. 'I just *can't* let you miss it!'

The view from the staff balcony was rather more inspiring than Jeff had made it sound. They were nine floors up and the lights of the town lay below them like scattered jewels. In the distance they could see the lovely Vale of Evesham. Jeff looked down at her.

'Are you warm enough?'

'Yes. It's very mild, thank you.' She hoped desperately that he hadn't noticed the trembling she found so hard to control. 'Well?' she said, the tension she felt giving a sharp edge to her voice. 'Are you going to tell me what it's all about?'

'Ah yes – Jane and Richard. Well, a while ago she confided to me that Richard seemed to be taking her for granted. She said she thought it was because they'd known each other for so long. Well, as you know, I'm very fond of little Jane and I didn't like to see her unhappy. I thought I might be able to help by making Richard see Jane through new eyes – *my* eyes. I began talking to him about her at every opportunity – saying what a super girl she was and how attractive etc. I think I even said at one point that I'd like a girl just like her myself.' He ran a hand through his hair. 'Well, I must have overdone it and the upshot was that Richard thought he might be standing in the way of a beautiful romance. He thought that Jane saw him merely as a comfortable habit and he'd better fade out and leave the way clear for me!' He looked at her wryly. 'Have you ever felt the biggest idiot in the world? I know I did when he told me that. If you hadn't drawn my attention to it, Megan, I'd have spoilt things for those two – maybe for good!'

She sighed. 'I know the feeling. I almost did something similar. So now Richard knows the truth – will he make it up with Jane?'

Jeff nodded. 'He's coming here tonight. It's to be a surprise, so don't say anything.' He picked up her ringless left hand and looked at it. 'You did it then?' he said quietly.

She drew her hand away. 'Yes – I did it.'

'Is that what you meant just now when

you said you almost did something similar?'

She nodded. 'Yes – but it's a very long and boring story, so don't ask me to tell you about it.' She tried to avoid his eyes. 'Shall we go back inside now? The others will be wondering where we are.' She made to walk past him but he caught her arm and held it fast.

'Wait, Megan. So now you're free again. What are you going to do?'

'I really haven't given the matter much thought,' she said. 'Except that I may look for another job. Mistakes have a way of hanging around like ghosts.'

'I don't believe in ghosts,' he said. 'They're in the past. People like you and me – we belong in the present and the future.'

She looked up at him. 'I may be mistaken, but I don't see you as a far-thinking person. I thought you believed in letting the future take care of itself.'

Without warning he grasped her shoulders and pulled her towards him, kissing her hard. 'That's the future I'm thinking of, Megan,' he said. 'Melting that icy shell of yours and getting down to the warm softness that I know is underneath it.' His arm slid round her, drawing her close and he kissed her again, his lips hard and demanding. 'Unwind, Megan,' he whispered urgently. 'Let yourself go. You're a lovely girl and you're driving me crazy, can't you see that?' He looked down at her and gave her a gentle shake. 'I know you don't really hate me, Meg. What is it that holds you back?' He held her close – so close that she could hardly breathe and her heart pounded wildly as his lips came down on hers again, this time gently, exploringly. At last, her hands against his chest, she pushed till he loosened his hold slightly, looking down at her with puzzled eyes.

'What *is* the matter? Tell me, damn it!'

She gave a shuddering sigh. 'It doesn't matter. Just leave me alone, Jeff. I'm not like you. I can't play at love the way you do. For me it would have to be real. That was why I couldn't go on with my engagement to David. When I give my love to someone it will have to be wholeheartedly and for keeps.'

For a long moment he stared at her, then he dropped his hands to his sides. 'Well – thanks for telling me anyway.'

There was an air of finality about his words that chilled her heart and she opened her mouth to say something else. But at that moment another couple came out onto the balcony and the words died on her lips.

'Shall we go in?' she said in a whisper. He

nodded gravely.

Back in the midst of the revelry Megan stood on the edge of the dance floor and watched, feeling that she had no part in any of it. David and Celia were dancing together, eyes only for each other, happiness in every movement. Richard Neale had arrived and sat holding Jane's hand and talking earnestly to her. Her cheeks were pink and her eyes shone as she listened. On the other side of the room Julia Simms was with her new boy friend, looking up into his eyes as glowingly as she had once looked into Jeff's. Megan crept away to the cloakroom. No one would notice if she left now. She would leave a note for Jane who would quite clearly be taken home by Richard anyway.

Down in the car park she unlocked the car and slid gratefully into its closed darkness, feeling safe at last. Jeff had not followed her as she had suspected he might. This time her message seemed to have got across to him – but the thought gave her no comfort. She tried to feel glad that everyone else's problems were sorting themselves out so nicely but her heart was too heavy even for that. She drove home through the mellow, moonlit night with a tight knot of tears in her throat. Why did her life seem so desolate suddenly? Why was everything so wretchedly complicated?

CHAPTER TEN

The following week Megan spent most of her time with Jane; partly to keep out of the way of Celia and David, but mostly to take Jane's mind off her coming ordeal. She had arranged to spend Wednesday night at the flat so that she could take Jane into Brinkdown with her on Thursday morning when she went in to the combined clinic.

The girls got up to find that the morning post had brought a card from Richard wishing Jane good luck and Megan could tell by the look on Jane's face as she read the message inside that he had written something special for her. Jane had been a different person since the night of the hospital dance, though she had not said a great deal about it to Megan – just that their misunderstanding was over and things were as before between them.

As they drove through the heavy morning traffic Megan could tell that her friend was nervous. Her face was pale and she had little to say. Megan tried to keep up the flow of conversation, chatting about everything she could think of, from the weather to the latest fashions to take Jane's mind off the twenty-four hours to come.

They arrived at the hospital at half-past-nine and as the clinic didn't begin until ten-thirty Megan had time to see Jane admitted. They sat together as the familiar forms were filled in, then Jane went up to the path lab for the routine blood test. It was here as Megan sat waiting outside that she saw a familiar tall figure striding towards her down the corridor.

'Hello! What are you doing here so early?' he said.

She gulped, wishing her cheeks wouldn't burn so. 'I came with Jane, she's being admitted,' she told him. 'She's very nervous and I thought I might be a comfort, but I'm beginning to wonder if I'm not making things worse for her!'

He nodded. 'I know. It's a job to know what to do for the best. At least the business with Richard seems to have sorted itself out. That must have gone a long way towards making her happier.'

Jane emerged from the path lab and Jeff grasped her arm firmly. 'Right young lady, you can take that worried look off your

226

pretty little face right now!' he said with mock severity. 'I don't allow it while I'm in charge. Why, you'll have Mr Oldershaw thinking I've been frightening the life out of you and you know I'm trying hard to make a good impression on him, don't you?' He lifted up her chin with one finger. 'Now – let's see that smile.'

Jane managed a smile for him. 'Oh, Jeff, I wish you were going to do the op'. I always feel so safe with you,' she said.

He laughed. 'Well! You're the first girl who ever said that to me! I'm not at all sure that it's a compliment. It makes me feel positively *old!*'

They all three laughed and the tension was broken. Jeff took a quick look round and bent to kiss Jane's cheek.

'You'll get me struck off, you wicked girl!' He pinched her cheek. 'Don't worry. I'll be there to see you through. You'll be fine. See you later, Megan.' And he hurried away down the corridor. Jane looked at Megan.

'Isn't he wonderful? I think he's the most gorgeous man I know – next to Richard, of course.'

Megan looked away as she felt her cheeks burning again. 'He's all right, I suppose,' she mumbled.

She saw Jane comfortably settled in the ward and then went off to attend the combined clinic, having first obtained Sister's permission to look in on Jane during the lunch break. When she came back there was a huge basket of red roses beside Jane's bed with a note from Richard. On it were just four words: 'I love you – Richard.' And it was clear from the expression on Jane's face that her apprehension had cleared quite a lot.

'I feel I can face anything now,' she confided to Megan. 'How could he ever have thought that I loved someone else?'

She told Megan that she had already had the routine check with the anaesthetist and everything was now, as she put it, 'all systems go'.

'I'm the first on the list in the morning, so Sister tells me, so I shan't have to hang around all morning waiting for my turn.' She grinned. 'Think of me starving when you're tucking into your bacon and eggs tomorrow morning!'

Megan was pleased to see her so much more cheerful. 'Would you like me to visit tonight, or will Richard be coming?' she asked. Jane reached for her hand.

'He will, but he may not be able to get

here until almost the end of visiting time. There's a staff meeting at school, so please come too, won't you? If it's not too much of a bore.'

Megan squeezed her hand reassuringly. 'Of course it isn't a bore! I'll be here. Have a good rest this afternoon and I'll see you later.'

But when she arrived at the hospital that evening, her arms full of magazines and paperbacks she could see from the ward doorway that Richard was, in fact, there. She was just about to turn away when a voice spoke behind her.

'He managed to skip his meeting so that he could be with Jane.'

She turned to see Jeff at her elbow, but his brow was furrowed as he looked down the ward at the two heads so close together. Megan looked up at him enquiringly.

'Is anything wrong? You look worried.'

He chewed his lip. 'Come up to the canteen and have a coffee with me.'

She hesitated. 'I wanted Jane to have these.' She held out the books.

'Leave them in Sister's office,' he said abruptly. 'Jane has Richard, she'll be all right. And when he goes she should be getting her rest ready for tomorrow.' He looked at her, noting that the look of doubt was still on her face. 'Oh, come on, Megan. I need company right at this moment – in fact, I need *you!*'

Her heart gave a painful jerk as she looked at him. 'All right,' she said and followed him to Sister's office, her heart beating fast.

In the canteen they settled at a corner table with their coffee. It was quiet and most of the other tables were empty. Jeff looked thoughtful as he stirred his cup.

'What is it, Jeff?' Megan asked again. 'Is there something wrong with Jane – something she doesn't know about?'

He shook his head. 'Lord, no – nothing like that. It's just that I had a message from Gloucester half an hour ago. Mr Oldershaw has been taken ill with some kind of food poisoning – he won't be coming tomorrow.'

'Oh, poor man, I'm so sorry.' Megan looked at him. 'So that means you'll be doing the operation after all.'

He sighed. 'You've got it. I told Richard when he arrived. He'll be telling Jane.'

Megan smiled. 'She'll be glad. It's what she wanted.'

But he shook his head angrily. 'She wouldn't if she knew how I felt about it!'

She frowned. 'I don't understand. You said there was nothing else wrong – no complications, so why are you so worried? It's quite straightforward, isn't it?'

'No, damn it, it isn't!' He stared at her. 'How would you like to have your vocal cords operated on by a surgeon who was scared stiff?'

Megan stared at him in disbelief. Brash, confident Jeff Maitland, admitting to being scared stiff. She shook her head. 'But you must have done this operation lots of times before, surely?' she said.

He pushed a hand through his hair impatiently. 'A few times, yes, and it's always been one I hated doing. Every surgeon has his pet hates and this is mine. It's not only that though, it's the fact that it's Jane. She thinks I'm some sort of God – that I can do no wrong. Suppose I make a mess of it – leave her without a voice at all?'

She reached across the table and covered his hand with hers. 'You're not to talk like that, Jeff. You know as well as I do that it simply won't happen.'

But he shook his head. 'No man – no human being is infallible, Megan. We all make mistakes. If only it wasn't little Jane!'

He looked tired and drawn and Megan felt her heart twist with love for him. 'Can I help, Jeff?' she asked quietly. 'If there's anything I can do to help – anything at all–'

He looked up at her, putting his hand on top of the one that covered his and pressing it lightly. 'Come home with me now, Meg,' he said in a low voice. 'Stay with me tonight.'

Startled, she looked at him for a long moment, then drew her hand from between his. 'Jeff – is this some kind of trick? Because if it is–' she broke off as she saw his expression. 'All right – I'll come – for a while at least.'

It wasn't until they got to the flat that she remembered she hadn't eaten. She discovered he hadn't either so they made a meal together in his neat kitchen. Afterwards, she telephoned Celia to tell her not to wait up for her. She found it rather embarrassing explaining where she was and why and when she eventually replaced the receiver she turned and caught Jeff with a grin on his face. She immediately felt her colour rise.

'I'm glad you find it so amusing, listening to me telling a whole fistful of white lies!' she said defensively.

He smiled lazily. 'It was only that you found it *necessary* that I found so amusing,' he said. 'Do you really think that Celia would be so shocked if you told her that you were staying over with me?'

'It would have been rather difficult for me to tell her the circumstances, wouldn't it?' she said pointedly.

The grin vanished from his face at once. 'No – you're right. I just can't resist teasing you, can I? I'm sorry, Meg.'

'I've told you before,' she said, stacking the plates from the table. 'Don't call me Meg!'

He followed her through to the kitchen and picked up a tea towel. 'Why is it that you hate to be called Meg?' he asked. 'And who is this mysterious person who has the honour of using it?'

She coloured. 'Never mind. It doesn't matter.'

They washed up in silence for a while, then he said: 'Tell me what happened over your engagement to David, Meg – an.'

She sighed. 'Do I have to?'

He threw down the cloth. 'Well we have to talk about *some* darned thing, don't we? I thought you were going to try and help me not to let tomorrow prey on my mind!'

She picked up the cloth and hung it up neatly, then put the clean dishes away in the cupboard. 'Well,' she said slowly, 'I told you that I thought David was someone else, didn't I? Because of something that happened in the past – to someone I'm very fond of – I wanted to teach him a lesson. Then I found out that he wasn't the person at all. That's all there is to it. At first I was afraid I'd done a lot of harm, then I discovered that he was deeply in love with Celia, so all ended well.' She looked at him. 'Satisfied?'

He frowned. 'I'm not sure. It sounds like one of those plots from an Italian opera – clear as mud! But if you say it's all right, then I suppose it is. Tell me something, Megan: Have *you* ever been in love?'

She stared straight back at him, her eyes bright. 'Have *you?*'

He sighed. 'I can see that it's going to be one of those evenings! Look, Megan, there's no need to be so jumpy. I'm quite a harmless bloke really. Come and sit down. I'll show you my photograph album. Even you couldn't detect an ulterior motive in that!'

As he turned the pages of the album Megan gradually saw the pattern of his life unfold. The smiling couple standing in front of a wooden bungalow were, he told her, the uncle and aunt who had brought him up; the two fair-haired laughing children, he and his sister, Debbie. There were snaps of dogs and ponies, groups of other children with whom they had shared their first studies; Jeff and Debbie again as lanky teenagers tanned and fit-looking from the open air. Then college groups in which a new figure stood between them – Peter, the young man whom Debbie had eventually married. The last photos in the album were of Jeff's aunt and uncle again, older now and standing on the front porch of the beautiful new house they had built for their retirement. With them was another couple, arms around each other's waists as they smiled into each other's eyes.

'Debbie and Peter.' Jeff pointed. 'I had a letter the other day, from Aunt Freda, she said that Debbie is expecting her first baby, around Christmas.'

Megan turned to look at him. 'That's great news. You'll be an uncle yourself. Aren't you pleased?'

He shrugged and snapped the album shut. 'Let's talk about you for a change. Have you any family?'

'None to speak of,' she told him. 'My parents are both dead. Dad when I was still at school and Mum a few years ago.'

'No sisters or brothers?' he asked, his head on one side.

'Only an adopted one – well, a cousin really. We grew up as sisters.'

'Is she like you?'

She laughed. 'Like me? Heavens no! Caroline couldn't be more opposite – she's–' She broke off as she realised that the name had slipped out. He looked at her.

'What's the matter?'

'Nothing – nothing at all,' she stammered. 'It's just that it's terribly hot in here. May I have a drink of water, please?'

'Of course.' He got up and went to the kitchen, a puzzled look on his face. When he came back she had managed to regain her composure, but he looked at her oddly as he handed her the glass.

'Did you say Caroline?' he asked. 'It couldn't possibly have been Caroline Streatfield, could it – who used to teach at the village school at Little Avedon?'

She was about to deny it all, wild panic rising inside her like an erupting volcano. He looked at her scarlet face and pointed a triumphant finger.

'Of course – you're *that* Meg! She called you it! Why didn't you say so before? I–' He broke off as a thought occurred to him. 'Wait a minute. You said – something happened to someone of whom you were very fond and you came here to teach that person a lesson.' He frowned. 'And you thought that David

Lattimer was that person!'

Megan got up from the settee and began to back towards the door but he continued to look puzzled, his brows knotted with concentration. Suddenly he snapped his fingers.

'It was because of the house, wasn't it? Because of Grey's Lodge? That was why you were in such a state that night when I happened to say that I once lived there. The man you were gunning for was *me!*' He threw back his head and roared with laughter. 'Oh, my poor Meg! What a shock that must have been! I bet you thought you were onto a soft touch with David. His good nature and easy-going manners would've been a pushover for you wouldn't they? You would have ground him under your heel like a worm, wouldn't you – for hurting your poor little cousin. What a vindictive female you must be! More like an embittered virago than the lovely young woman you appear on the surface!' He grasped her wrist as she reached for the door handle. 'Not so fast! We've got some talking to do!' He pulled her, stumbling, over to the settee and pushed her into it. 'It seems to me that you might have taken the trouble to get to know that cousin of yours a bit better before you started taking fate into your own hands. I've never met anyone who needed protecting less than she did! If ever a girl could look after herself, she could! She very nearly had *me* all parcelled up and posted to the register office!'

Megan took a deep breath. 'Jeff – before you say anything else I want you to know that everything you've said so far is absolutely true. I was a fool. I interfered and I got what was coming to me. I've gone through quite a lot already, so cool down a little will you?'

The angry look left his eyes and he let out his breath on a sigh, shaking his head and looking at her speculatively as he sat down beside her on the settee. 'I suppose that looked at in one light, what you did could be interpreted as loyalty,' he said slowly. 'That certainly sounds more like you.'

She smiled at him wryly. 'Thank you for giving me the benefit of the doubt. It was like this: Caroline came to live with us when we were both five. Her parents had been killed in an air crash on the way home from visiting a relative in Canada. She was more of a baby than me, tiny and fragile, timid and lost. I understood that she was an orphan even though I was young and, right from the first, I made it my business to look after her. At school I fought all her battles, I helped her with her sums and her reading – generally mothered her. And that's been the pattern ever since. These habits die hard, you know. It was only when I came here and heard other people's opinions of her that I saw the effects of my mothering; the more unattractive trait in her character caused by my over-protection of her.'

He grinned. 'In other words, her over-powering bossiness.'

She nodded. 'She's the first to admit it now. You see, since she moved up to Scotland she's found a man who loves her enough to make her change. They're to be married soon. I've seen them together and, believe me, there'll be nothing hen-pecked about Angus.'

'Well – I'm glad to hear it.' He looked at her for a long moment. 'When you love someone you wade right in, don't you, Meg? I can't think of anyone else who would involve herself so deeply in someone else's life.'

She bit her lip and looked away. 'Caroline was always special to me – rather like your sister was to you. But people grow up and change. There comes a time when one must let go. The trouble is that we don't always recognise that time when it comes. I learned it the hard way.'

He nodded thoughtfully. 'So – now that all the problems are solved what happens next?'

'I suppose it's time I gave some serious thought to my own life,' she said. ''Till now I've been too busy trying to organise Caroline's. I've only just realised that I have a future too.'

'And what would you like it to be?' he asked.

His eyes were looking intently into hers and she could hardly bear it. She jumped up from the settee and looked at her watch. 'Good heavens! Just look at the time. Right now we should both be thinking of going to bed!' The moment the words were out she bit her lip, her cheeks flaming at the implication.

His lips twitched and his eyes twinkled as he stood up to face her. 'Why, Miss Lacey – I believe you're making improper suggestions to me!' he said mischievously.

She smiled in spite of her embarrassment. 'You know perfectly well what I meant. You have a very heavy day ahead of you tomorrow – so if you wouldn't mind running me back to the hospital I can get my car.'

He shook his head. 'But you promised to stay.'

She stared at him. 'I said for a while,' she said, her heart quickening.

He put his hands on her shoulders, looking down at her appealingly. 'Don't go, Meg. I don't want to be on my own tonight. A sympathetic, sensitive person like you should understand that.'

Her eyes flashed. 'You're laughing at me again! You're trying to make a fool of me to – to pay me back! Well, if you won't take me I shall just have to walk!' She tried to turn away, but his fingers held her like steel. 'It's all of two miles, it's raining and it's after midnight,' he said. 'And I'm not laughing at you. Far from it. Come on, Meg, just relax and settle down.'

'You're despicable!' she blazed at him. 'You tricked me into this – *why?*'

He looked down at her teasingly. 'Why does a man usually want to be alone with a girl?' Before she could answer he was kissing her. For a moment she struggled wildly, then she gave herself up to the melting feeling inside her, her knees turning to water and her head swimming dizzily. Her mind frantically tried to regain control of her emotions. It was an explosive situation. If she stayed here – if he kept on kissing her like this she would be lost – another victim like all the others. What was it Jane had said? 'You always know where you are with Jeff.' She was right. Heaven only knew he'd said it often enough: 'No close relationships.' That was all very well if you had a heart like a bullet!

But through all these thoughts she still clung to him helplessly, his lips warm on hers and his arms strong and hard around her. It was too late for sanity. Whatever was to happen, must happen. If she was to be hurt, then hurt she must be. There was no longer anything she could do about it.

'Oh, Meg, you're so sweet, so lovely,' he whispered. Then suddenly he put her from him, looking down at her, his mouth set in a firm line. 'You were right,' he said. 'I do have a heavy day tomorrow.' He took a deep breath. 'I'll get you some blankets. This settee converts into a bed. You'll be fine on that, won't you?'

He went away and returned a moment later with blankets and pillows, unfolded the settee, then stood back, looking at her a little sheepishly. 'Thank you for staying, Meg. I appreciate it. I really did need your company. Sleep well.' He bent and kissed her forehead then turned on his heel and left the room, closing the door firmly behind him.

Megan made up her bed slowly, a feeling of anticlimax overwhelming her. What had happened? How could he suddenly switch off like that? It just went to show how shallow he really was. But his kisses certainly hadn't seemed shallow and they haunted her dreams for the rest of the night.

When she woke she found a note on the table. It read: 'Darling Meg, you looked so sweet I hadn't the heart to wake you. I've left because I want to be at the hospital early. I'll send one of the porters round with your car. Please think of me – and Jane – today. Thank you for last night – Jeff.'

She looked at her watch. It was still only eight o'clock and she wondered if he had left to avoid seeing her. She got up, folded her blankets and restored her bed to its former shape, then she went into the kitchen. Jeff had made himself breakfast but washed up before he left. She made herself some toast and coffee, thinking of Jane as she ate it. She would be having her pre-med about now. The worrying would be over. She would be feeling pleasantly woosy and when she woke up it would all be over. Not for Jeff though. For him the ordeal was yet to come. Was he really as nervous as he said? Had he really needed her for that reason last night – or had it been merely a trick to get her up to the flat? If so, why had he suddenly cooled? Perhaps he didn't find her attractive after all. She sighed and pulled herself together. She too had a hard day's work ahead of her and she had promised to look in at the hospital at lunch time to see how the operation had gone. For a few hours she must try to put Jeff out of her mind. Then later still, out of her life altogether if she was to have that future she had promised herself.

The morning passed uneventfully and at lunch time she drove to the hospital, hurrying up to the ward, anxious to see how Jane was. As it was out of visiting hours she tapped on the door of Sister's office then put her head round the door. She knew Sister Blake quite well as she had often been up to the E.N.T. ward to work with patients.

'I wondered if Jane Lang had come back from the theatre yet,' she said.

Sister Blake smiled. 'She has and she's fine. I don't know whether you heard that Mr Oldershaw went down with food poisoning yesterday, so Mr Maitland did the operation,' she said. 'But everything went well and Jane should be fine, though of course she isn't allowed to use her voice for a short period and there will be some soreness at first.'

Megan beamed with relief. 'May I see her?'

Sister nodded. 'Just for a few minutes, though as I said she won't be able to talk to you. She may still be rather sleepy from the anaesthetic too.'

Jane opened her eyes and smiled as Megan sat down beside her bed. Megan held a finger to her lips.

'You mustn't try to speak. Sister tells me you're just fine – and Jeff did your op' after all, eh?'

Jane nodded, smiling happily and after a few minutes Megan saw that she had drifted off to sleep again. She crept out quietly, wondering where Jeff was and whether he had finished his list for the day.

Knowing that Richard would be sure to visit that evening and that Jane mustn't be overtired she bought fruit and a book of crossword puzzles and brought them back to the hospital with a note for Jane. She would have liked to congratulate Jeff but she didn't know where to find him, so after having a chat to Sister Blake she went on to her afternoon clinic at St Angela's school. She enjoyed working with the handicapped children and it pained her to think that she would soon have to say goodbye to them all.

As she drank her usual cup of tea in Molly Edwards' office afterwards the older woman remarked that she was looking better than she had last week.

'You've more colour today,' she said. 'Last week I was quite concerned for you. You looked as though you were sickening for something. This week you've quite a glow about you.'

Megan nodded. She knew the reason for it – she knew also that it would be short-lived.

Jane improved steadily and because the hospital needed the bed so badly Megan volunteered to move into Jane's flat and take care of her so that she could be discharged. Richard collected her on the following Saturday morning and by the time they arrived Megan had the little flat sparkling, fresh flowers everywhere and an appetising lunch prepared. Jane was still on her honour not to use her voice more than was absolutely necessary, but she was clearly finding it more and more difficult as the days went by.

It was a beautiful day and after lunch Richard suggested that he took Jane out for a drive in the country. They didn't invite Megan along but she hadn't expected them to. No doubt they had plans to make now that Jane was on the road to recovery and it would be good for them to spend a little time alone after meeting for days in a hospital ward.

When they had gone she washed up the lunch things and made some scones and a sponge for tea. She had just put them into the oven when there was a ring at the door bell. Hastily dusting the flour from her hands she went to answer it, but she caught her breath sharply when she saw that it was Jeff who stood on the threshold, a large bunch of flowers in his hand.

'Oh! I'm sorry but Jane's out. Richard has taken her for a run in the car,' she said.

He nodded. 'Then I'll come in and talk to you instead.' He stepped inside and handed the flowers to her. 'Maybe you could put these in water or something. I feel a real banana standing here holding them,' he said.

She took them from him. 'Of course.'

He followed her into the kitchen and watched as she filled a vase at the sink and began to unwrap the flowers. His eyes made her nervous and at last she said:

'I'm afraid they might be some time – all afternoon, in fact – so if there's anything else you have to do–'

'There isn't,' he said briefly.

'Oh.' She continued to arrange the flowers, then carried them through to the living room. 'Jane will enjoy them – they're lovely,' she said, glancing at him sideways.

'They are quite nice,' he observed. 'I got them from the little shop on the corner – do you know it? It's called Fleur d'Amour, or something fancy like that.'

'Yes – I believe I've passed it.'

An awkward silence developed between them and next time they spoke it was both at the same time. Megan laughed.

'What were you about to say?'

He shrugged. 'I just wondered if you knew the latest test score.'

She shook her head. 'No – but do put the radio on if you want to. I must go back to the kitchen. I was doing some baking.'

He stepped across the room in two strides and caught her wrist. 'Meg – why have you been avoiding me?'

Her heart began to thud. 'I haven't,' she lied.

He frowned. 'I think you have.'

'I – I wanted to see you on the day of Jane's op',' she told him. 'To congratulate you, but I thought you'd be busy. You did a fine job and I know Jane is very grateful.'

He shook his head impatiently. 'I didn't

come here to talk "shop", Meg. I came to talk to you.'

'I must go back to the kitchen,' she said breathlessly. 'Everything will be burned to a cinder.'

In the kitchen she took the scones from the oven and put the tray on the table. Jeff stood in the doorway, watching her.

'Did you know that you had a smear of flour on your nose?' he asked her.

She lifted her hand to brush it away and as she did so caught her wrist on the hot baking tray. *'Oh!'*

In an instant he had crossed the kitchen and taken her arm. 'What is it? Does it hurt?' He looked into her eyes. 'Oh Meg – darling, can't you see what you've done to me? I've been trying to contact you for days. I can't sleep for thinking about you. I've even lost my appetite!'

She pushed him away. 'Don't be ridiculous, Jeff. You're laughing at me again,' she said shakily.

But he held her fast, shaking his head. 'I've never been more serious in my life. I rang Celia at the cottage and she said you were here – after a lot of persuasion. Then I had to twist Richard's arm to get him to make sure you were here alone this afternoon.

You've no idea of the trouble I've gone to. Meg–' He looked deeply into her eyes and his own were the colour of deep water. 'Meg, I want you to know something and then – if it's what you want – I'll go away and never bother you again. You've achieved what you came here to do. You've got that revenge you wanted. You wanted to pay back the man who hurt your cousin's pride – well you succeeded.'

She stared at him. 'How? I don't see what you mean.'

'By making me fall in love with you, that's how, you little fool. And you did it without even trying! Oh, I *fancied* you at first, as I have so many others, then, all at once before I knew what had hit me it was love!' He took both her hands in his. 'That night at the flat – I was going to get you out of my system once and for all but when it came to the crunch I couldn't do it. You were too important to me. That was when I knew what I'd got myself into.' He shook his head. 'It hurts, Meg. I was wise to leave it alone.' He let go her hands. 'Right, now you can tell me to get lost.'

She gazed up at him in disbelief. Was this really happening or was she dreaming it? 'I – I know it hurts, Jeff,' she said softly, 'and as for getting my own back – it wasn't quite like that. I fell into my own trap – and I know very well how painful love can be. I've known for some time.' She reached up and put her arms round his neck.

He shook her gently. 'I was under the impression that you thought me a prize heel – the last person you'd ever fall for. Why did you go out of your way to make me think that?' he asked.

'Isn't it obvious? Your veto on close relationships,' she told him. 'I told you once that casual affairs were not my scene. It didn't alter the way I felt though.'

He looked down at her with a slightly comic expression. 'Then I suppose there's nothing for it but to ask you to marry me?'

She laughed. 'I'm afraid not.'

Suddenly his eyes were serious and he bent to kiss her, a long satisfying kiss. 'Here goes then,' he said as they drew apart. 'Please, Miss Lacey – will you marry me?'

She smiled. 'Are you quite sure you don't mind turning into – what did you call it? A "one-track turnip-head"?'

He laughed and pulled her close. 'Not as long as you're on the same track with me. Oh, and Megan, you taught me something else. It was something you said the other night when you were talking about Caroline. You said we have to learn when to "let go". It made me see how stupid and immature I'd been over Debbie and Peter and I thought – how would you fancy a honeymoon in Australia, helping me to get to know them all over again?'

'Oh, Jeff, I'd *love* it!'

For a long time no more words were spoken until a smell of burning reached their nostrils and Megan gave a little cry of dismay:

'Oh! My sponge!'

They both rushed to the oven and threw open the door only to see the smoking remains of the sponge cake inside. They looked at each other, then Jeff laughed.

'Well, I can't think of a better or more worthy cause for a sacrifice, can you?' He grinned at her. 'Believe it or not, you still have that streak of flour on your nose!'

She lifted her hand to wipe it away but he caught her fingers and raised them to his lips. 'No, don't. I want to remember you just as you are now.' He kissed her. 'I've a feeling I'm going to go on loving you for quite a long time, Megan Lacey – for a life-time, in fact, so I think you'd better marry me pretty soon.'

She buried her face – flour and all – against his shoulder. 'As soon as you like, darling,' she said happily.

The publishers hope that this book has given you enjoyable reading. Large Print Books are especially designed to be as easy to see and hold as possible. If you wish a complete list of our books please ask at your local library or write directly to:

Dales Large Print Books
Magna House, Long Preston,
Skipton, North Yorkshire.
BD23 4ND

This Large Print Book, for people
who cannot read normal print,
is published under the auspices of

THE ULVERSCROFT FOUNDATION